Us Fools Believing

Prose Series 47

Canadä

Guernica Editions Inc. acknowledges the support of
The Canada Council for the Arts.
Guernica Editions Inc. acknowledges the support of
the Ontario Arts Council.
Guernica Editions Inc. acknowledges the financial support of the
Government of Canada through the Book Publishing Industry
Development Program (BPIDP).

MIRIAM PACKER

US FOOLS BELIEVING

SHORT STORIES

GUERNICA
TORONTO·BUFFALO·LANCASTER (U.K.)
2000

Antonio D'Alfonso, editor

Guernica Editions Inc.

P.O. Box 117, Station P, Toronto (ON), Canada M5S 2S6

2250 Military Road, Tonawanda, N.Y. 14150-6000 U.S.A.

Gazelle, Falcon House, Queen Square, Lancaster LA1 1RN U.K.

Typeset by Selena.

Printed in Canada.

Legal Deposit — Fourth Quarter

National Library of Canada

Library of Congress Catalog Card Number: 00-107509

Canadian Cataloguing in Publication Data

Packer, Miriam

Us fools believing

(Prose series ; 47)

ISBN 1-55071-056-7

1. Title. II. Series

PS8581.A26U85 2000   C813'.54   C00-901139-0

PR9199.3.P276U85 2000

CONTENTS

PACING

The day they expel me from grade nine, Ma is smoking in front of the boob tube, with a cigarette in her hand and pom-pom slippers on her feet, watching the Opera-Win-Me Show. She hates it when I call it that, and I do it to get a rise out of her.

When I tell her they threw me out, she bites her lip and says nothing. I will give her this, though; she does put the remote on mute.

"You're in a deep puddie now," she says.

"I'll get a job."

She sucks in her breath. "You'll end up on the welfare, Lanie."

"That's where you've been," I snap, "you and Pa – wherever the hell he is."

That's when she smacks me, awful perfect timing she has. Thug-slap against my ear, so my back molars begin to ache.

"Don't you talk about your pa like that," she says. "You owe him respect; he brought you into this world."

That's the way she talks. Like the people on those talk shows.

Ma knows everything about those talk-show people, about their husbands and boyfriends and children, just like they're family.

Yesterday, out of nowhere, she says to me, "Should get me some flu shots, keep the bug out."

"Why now?" I say.

"I just should, is all," she says. "Kathie and Regis got

theirs last Friday." Kathie and Regis, the morning talk show hosts.

"Excuse me?" I go.

"Right on the television they got them. Oh, Regis made a fuss," she giggles. "You know Regis. But Kathie took it without no fuss. Women are stronger than men, Kathie says." Ma takes a sip of tea. "Cody's talking now," she says.

"Who's Cody?" I say, even though I know perfectly well that's Kathie Lee's child. Kathie Lee talks about her kid on her show all the time, and Ma goes gaga.

"Oh for goodness' sake," Ma says. "*You* know Cody."

I don't say anything. I just give her a you-dodo look, like she deserves. Dumb, talking about a movie star's kid like it's her own.

Anyways, Ma goes on talking to me now, like she didn't almost give me a concussion a minute ago, smacking me upside my head.

"Now you got caught," she says, "and they thrown you out altogether. You'll be a dummy all your life." She looks straight ahead, like she's talking to a camera. "I done everything to keep her in school, and now this."

"Hey, Ma! Who you talking to?" I say. "I'm right here, remember?"

She jerks her head to look at me. "You'll end up with nothing. There's no jobs for people without their grade twelves."

"I got news for you. There's hardly any jobs for anybody anyways." I do my best fuck-you wiggle across the living room, and walk away.

"You should of stayed in school," she shouts at the back of my head, "where they cared about your future."

"Don't you worry about me!" I yell back without turning

round. "Maybe I'll die or something. Then you'll be sorry you hit me."

"My nerves," Ma says in a shaky voice.

Truth is nobody ever looked at me in school – but I never told her that. Every time I put up my hand, which was not like too darned often, Mr. Clarkson pretended he didn't see me. He made this shadow move over his eyes, like Grampa's cataracts. He let on he couldn't see my hand poking up there, and my face going red.

Clarkson lives three streets away from us, and he knows Pa from way back, before Pa left Ma.

Three streets away may not sound very far, but it's like a different country. That's where the real houses start. Duplexes and bungalows, with nice curtains in the windows and some grass in front. Where Clarkson lives, people own their places and have jobs and stuff. Not like on our block, where half of them are on welfare, and nobody pays their rent in time.

Anyways, Clarkson remembers Pa from when he spent his days at Al's Soda near Clarkson's street, and would sit over coffee and talk too loud, blast the government and the welfare system, and blast Ma for killing his dreams.

In class one day, Clarkson sat in on our discussion groups about family. He came to sit with my group just when I was telling a pack of lies about Pa working for the government and being away on government business. Clarkson had this tight smile, and his eyes went slanted. "I believe I've encountered your dad, Lanie," he said. "He used to frequent Al's Soda, did he not?"

Clarkson chuckled on his spit.

For sure he knew my armpits had gone to slush, and my tongue was sticking to the roof of my mouth.

"A critical man," Clarkson said. "Admirable quality, that."

Clarkson never let on he was poking fun at Pa, but I knew what he thought of us. Junk is what he thought of us. Like day-old bread. Nothing like Alexandra Demers who lives in one of those fancy-curtain places near his house, and her mother sends home-made stuff for us to treat on in class. Clarkson never goes blind on Alexandra or her friends when they put their hands up.

I've never told Ma any of that. She's too kiss-ass to understand. She figures guys like Clarkson are too smart to be mean. That's how much *she* knows about life. Like nothing.

Anyways, it's just like I'm going to school every morning. I get up just as early. Only difference is now I don't have to face Clarkson and Alexandra and them. I just put on one of my three straight skirts and a sweater and head out for the mall.

Ma hardly talks to me these days, and that's okay.

When I get to the mall, I go right to the bathroom. I take time with my eye shadow, put on thick purple and top it with pink. I don't skimp on the lipstick either. I put on the heels I have in my purse, and I'm on.

I take myself over to the Dunkin' Donuts counter, and put one high-heeled leg over the other so there's leg showing right up to my crotch. I order myself a fresh cruller and coke for breakfast. Cruller and pop sends the sweet right through my veins, makes me feel good. From the corner of my eye, I catch all the nut-cases on their stools watching my legs and sneaking glances up to my crotch and dribbling spit into their coffee, they want me so bad. I won't always be sitting on these stools, either. While I'm chewing my cruller, I can see myself making it big like Madonna. Who knows? One day, with these legs and my voice and stuff, I could find myself on the

Arsenio Hall Show (Arsenio Hole, she calls him; Arse-Hole for short, she says, because she likes Oprah and Sally better).

Afternoons at the mall, to change the mood, I pin my hair up, and visit the lingerie department. Turns my temp up, all those fancy brassieres and short silk petticoats chock full of lace. Jesus, I love those.

First time I get the nerve to take a few into the dressing room at Eaton's, I almost go nuts. It gives me a fit to see how drop-dead good I look.

Next morning I go back, and try on a purple with tiny pink flowers, and then I go for this sweet colour called Raspberry Blush.

There's nobody to bother me in Eaton's. They're short of salespeople these days. I take what I want, and try it on, and check myself out in the mirror, and bring it back.

"You could call Mr. Clarkson and make an apology about playing hookey," she says to me one day. "You know you need an education."

"Excuse me?" I say, and I beat my eyelashes, like a thousand times. "I don't want to get an education, okay? I've got things to do."

"Everyone needs an education," Ma says.

"Then you go and get one," I say.

Next thing I know, she's going back to school. Well, not school exactly, to a learning centre. She's heard about it on television. They tell you it's your second chance, that it opens doors for those who missed it.

One morning, she's dressed up in this navy-blue rayon suit she bought from Zeller's, a navy purse she's kept in plastic for about a hundred years, and pumps she's had for a billion. She's actually leaving Opera-Win-Me and the whole lot of them behind. It throws me, I'll tell you. I never expected her to get off that couch.

It feels creepy with the T.V. gone dead, and me left behind her, like I'm the one sending her off.

Nights, she sits at the kitchen table and concentrates on copying things out of the little books she brings home. It's adult learners like herself wrote them. Thin books with titles like *The Way Out* and *How I Won*. She sticks her tongue out the side of her mouth when she writes, and she erases a lot, and calls me Hon, something she hasn't called me in about a thousand years. She tells me about the talks they have in class, and the words she's learning. Words like fulfilment and empowerment. Control: that's a big one.

The first time it happens to me, it's not like I'm doing it. I've tried on so many, my cheeks are flushed, and I'm getting hungry, and think I'd better go home.

Anyways, I'm trying on a petticoat when it happens. The raspberry-blush stays on my back; I pull my sweater over it and put my coat on, and walk out of the store.

The petti is cool and silky and perfect against my skin; I wear it when I watch Arsenio, and I can swear he's looking right at me. I go to bed wearing only that.

This morning, I lifted my fifth set of lace panties and matching push-up bra.

I'm taking orders from my friends now, Millie and Trish and Pat. I meet them at Al's, and we do business.

Millie likes purple; I'm fixing up her trousseau, she jokes. She laughs so hard, she spurts Coca-Cola through her nose. So far I've gotten her a purple bra and mauve panties and opaque purple tights. She's offered to pay me half the regular price, but I won't take it.

"Don't get yourself caught," Trish says to me, and I tell her to chill out.

"Nobody's going to catch me," I tell her. "The salesladies are in the back, taking inventory or something."

The stealing is only temporary, though. Problem is I can't stop. It's only temporary, but I'm running crazier than ever.

I've even moved into sweaters, though it's harder to lift a sweater than a bra. A sweater is bulkier, and you can't slip it into your purse. But you can't stay in one place, is what I say. You got to make your way up sometimes.

I think of Ma's face, looking so flushed, and Ma talking big words like power and control, and my fingers get hot and I grab for another. It's a thing that happens; it takes over.

Until the day I come home, and she's sitting at the kitchen table, crying. Her books are on the floor, spread out like a broken puzzle where she dropped them.

She's crying so hard I see one bubbled tear coming out of her nose. It's gross to see, but it kind of makes me feel like crying too.

They had a class discussion, she tells me, and everyone talked about what they expected from the course. Lots of women said they had come to the centre just to get out of the house, have somewhere to go.

Not Ma, though. She said she had come to the centre to get herself a good-paying job, and she would not stop till she got one. "A respectable job that will get us a new life, is what I'm after," she said.

Ma started hiccuping tears. "Everyone in the group clapped for me, Lanie. But something happened to that teacher's face when I said that; it went all worried. She asked me to stay after class to talk."

First thing the teacher told Ma was not to get carried

away. "Many learners never do find jobs, Mrs. Sills," the teacher said. "Not with the economic situation the way it is. What the centre can do for you is help you feel good about mastering something."

Ma cannot talk much after she tells me that. All she manages to say is she is never going back.

"Piss on them," Ma says, first time I heard her using that word. "Piss on the whole bunch – Oprah and Sally and Kathie Lee too."

"Why them?" I ask, surprising the hell out of myself because I'm the one hated her thinking they were God.

"Learning centres and talk-show people are all the same," Ma says. "They get us fools believing we can make our lives better, when it isn't any of it true. They're the ones wearing the fancy clothes and making the good money, and we're the fools listening."

"It's not the same at the learning centre, though," I say.

"Oh, yes it is," Ma hisses. "They're not fancy like the T.V. ladies, but it's the same. They're the ones with the fine jobs, and we're the fools keeping them there. They never even mean for us to get work. There ain't no jobs to get."

"They taught you to read pretty good," I say, and I feel pretty dumb the minute I say it.

"Hah!" Ma says. "You're the one thought I looked stupid using those big words."

"Well," I mutter, "it's something to do, like. At least you got to wear your Zeller's dress to school."

"Hah!" Ma says. "Double hah!" And she closes the subject.

So there's nothing for me to do eventually, but go back and apologise to Clarkson and get myself back into school.

This is how it happens.

Ma sits by the window, looking like somebody died. She hardly eats and it's got me worried. I make her a sandwich, and she nibbles a bit, but she doesn't eat it. She just does not perk up.

So I figure there's only one way to straighten things out. I get myself over to school and make a big deal about apologising to Clarkson about playing hookey. I throw him a lot of reasons, and Clarkson goes for it. I tell him I have had troubles on my mind; personal problems of an emotional nature, is what I say. He likes the sound of that. I tell him I was having an identity crisis, and Clarkson's eyes go big when I use those words.

I tell him that I wasn't motivated, but that I got my motivation back now. I throw him a kiss-ass line about how I know he's very understanding, and he just eats that up.

So I'm back in school, and first thing I do is get myself a seat right up front where Clarkson has to take notice when my hand goes up. I tell him my eyes are bad, and that I concentrate better when I'm up front, and he has no choice but to sit me exactly where I want to be. That's empowerment, I figure.

I put up my hand in the morning and pretty much keep it there all day, giving Clarkson lots of hot-shot answers. It gives me a charge each time I give a good answer, using some big word I've picked up from Ma. Like the feeling I get out of eating crullers and coke, only better. It's a feeling carries me over from one day to the next, instead of lasting maybe an hour.

Ma still isn't looking too glad, and she still doesn't turn on the television. I haven't seen her taking her books out of the closet. I don't ask about the learning centre anymore though, or let on I think she should go back. Not yet, it's not the time.

Yesterday, I wrote a composition for my social studies class on the topic "a personal struggle." All about how I found something I like, and how it belongs to me. Pure corn, but I showed it to Ma, and she cried kind of good. Not the real sad kind of crying she's been doing lately – something better. Crying with a kick to it, if you know what I mean. Crying with an upper.

Today, she got me a red loose-leaf binder as a present. So I took out the raspberry blush petticoat I stole, and wrapped it in pink tissue paper, and gave it to Ma, just like it was a proper present and I bought it especially for her. It is a present, matter-of-fact, because it was my favourite one, and I won't be going back for anymore. That's the end of that.

She looks real nice in it. I caught her trying it on later when she thought I wasn't looking.

Something in my head tells me one of these days I'm going to catch her taking her books out of the closet, and putting her Zeller's suit on and sneaking back to the centre. Maybe just taking her books out; that would be a start.

I would like to tell her that – to read her books for a while, just for starters, while she's sitting by the window. But I've got to be careful what I say.

Pace. That's another word I use in class these days to throw old Clarkson, and show off for Alexandra and them.

I'm pacing myself with Ma. If I don't push her too much, if I don't move in on her all at once, in a big rush like, she might figure it out eventually by herself.

She might figure out that the real good part is the buzz in your ears, and your stomach doing cartwheels, when your hand shoots up and you say the answer out loud and you got it right. You got the answer good, and it belongs to you.

For the time being, there's no going further than that.

WOMAN-EYES

There's a whole pack of us crazies up here on the ward – about thirty of us, altogether – but I don't spend a whole lot o'time with most of 'em. Not cause I think I'm better or anythin' like that, see – but most of 'em, they got them shades pulled down over their eyes, and it just ain't no use. You can't get anything goin' with anybody in the way of some kinda decent conversation. Ain't nobody home, if you know what I mean. Ya start talking to someone around here – ya realize the cat's tuned in to some other kinda music. He ain't hearin' you at all.

I remember my mama sayin' to me when I'd get on her nerves. "Boy, I'm warnin' you now – one more time, and I'm gonna knock you silly." It always seemed strange to me when she'd say that; I always wondered how you could turn anyone silly by knockin 'em upside their head, ya know. It's only since I got in here, I figured out the real meanin' behind that. The drugs they hand out up here just knock folks silly, I'm tellin' ya. It plain turns 'em into sone kinda strange, grinnin' fools.

There's guys walkin' around here never talk, they got these dead faces on 'em – some just kinda closin' their eyes and just standin' in one spot all day long, and some kinda scuffin' their feet like there's tar attached to their shoes holdin' 'em down. They've been knocked silly, that's what it is, right down to the soles o' their feet. The drugs do that to them, that's what I think.

Me, I'm on four elavil pills a day – and compared to the

kinda drugs I was doin' before I came in here, that's easy street. I got my head together, lemme tell ya. I know what's goin' on.

I'm a musician just takin' some time out in this place. I'm in here to beat a small drug-pushin' rap – and the way I got my foot in the door, the head doctor who was seein' me before the bust said I had to come in here to come down from the drugs. That saved my skin. I'll tell ya. This ain't paradise, but it ain't the hell o' prison either.

Anyway, I spend my time in here with a few who still got their lights on. There's Dana, for one. She's got all kinds o' trouble with eatin', and she sure gets strung out sometimes, scared o' gettin' some fat on her bones. She near about died from that skinny disease before she got in here, and I can see she ain't finished with that starvin' program yet. Not by a long shot.

"Dana," I tell her, "girl, you could do with a little fat on your bones, believe me. What ya got hangin' around your arms is a whole loose mess o' chicken skin, girl. I'm tellin' it to you straight. It ain't a pretty sight, woman. Near about spoils my breakfast, sometimes."

"Rome," Dana says – she calls me Rome instead o' Jerome, and I don't mind, "Rome, you want my toast and jam? Take it fast so Eyes can't see." It happens every time. Dana gets me to eat her food, and if I can sneak it fast enough, I do. Just as long as the big nurse Miss Cobb don't see. Miss Cobb is Eyes – that's what we call her, her and the other nurses, but she's the quickest of 'em all. She's Eyes Number One, and if she catches Dana givin' her food away to me or flushin' it down the toilet like she sometimes does, or hidin' it in her pants, or throwin' it up on purpose with her fingers down her throat, there's hell to pay. They got Dana on some kinda trainin' program in here –conditioning, they call it –

and the idea is if she's been messin' up on her food and not eatin' right, they take away one of her privileges. Like maybe they won't let her have no visitors for a week, or they won't let her come to the day-room or somethin' like that.

Dana goes haywire when they won't let her mother come like she does every day, though I can't figure out why. They end up fightin' every time she comes anyway as far as I can see, with Dana cussin': "Leave me alone, Ma – just leave me alone just go and die or somethin', you drive me crazy." That's what happens every darn time her mama comes, but Dana needs her to just keep comin' anyway. She goes crazy if they take away her visiting privileges for a week.

Me, I don't get strung out if they take anythin' away from me. I got my friends on the outside, I got my music inside, and nothin' in here makes me lose my cool.

But anyway, most o' the time we don't get caught, Dana and me, and we have us a good time too. Dana keeps on the look-out for Eyes, or maybe she'll leave her food tray and go ask Eyes real quiet-like if she thinks there's lots o' potassium in bananas. And while she's doin' that, I'll slip my little finger around a half-slice o' whole wheat bread and flick it onto my plate, and then I'll eat two halves together like a toast sand-wich – and by the time Dana gets back, all her toast is gone, there's only a little bit o' egg left on her plate, and we're both feelin' happy.

Dana and me laugh about those therapy groups we have to go to once a week 'cause they're some kinda joke. There's six of us in our group. Dana, me, Mrs. Bloom (she's a sweet old lady, got all her marbles too), Mr. Archer, Mrs. Renshaw, and old Eddy. Miss Cobb runs our group herself. She tries to get us talkin' in here. Every time she goes through the same routine. She asks us to pull up our chairs in a circle, but that never works.

Eddy sits off in the corner, always. He's got his favourite leather chair back there, and he hangs onto it. Sometimes he sits with his head in his hands and leans forward, like he's thinkin' real hard. Other times, he keeps rockin' back and forth, like there's some kinda beat he's tuned into – and he just keeps movin' to it. But he don't get into no circle no-how, and he sure don't talk like Miss Cobb wants him to. The only thing Eddy ever says is "group-group-group" after Miss Cobb says it, or "talk-talk-talk" when she says it, just like some kinda parrot.

Mrs. Renshaw walks around the room a lot, like she's at some fancy garden party. She's one high-class lady, been to a lotta fancy parties in her day, wears some pretty fine rags even if she does spend every day just hangin' around the smelly day-room like the rest of us. She talks like she's some kinda movie star. Ain't no way Miss Cobb can get her to sit down and talk about f-ee-lings. Mrs. Renshaw's on the go.

"Well, now," Miss Cobb says in that particular big nurse voice. "What shall we discuss today?" She turns to Lady Renshaw. "What's on your mind, Mrs. Renshaw?"

Mrs. Renshaw sort o' moves around, like those high-falutin' white women waltzin' around a ballroom at those gigs we used to do at a fancy dinner club now and then.

"Well, my dear," Renshaw says, "I am frightfully worried about the dinner party Jonathan and I have organized. For the first of the month. I do want everything to be perfect, don't you see?"

Cobb tries to get her back on track just a little, but after a while, she lets it go.

"Mrs. Renshaw, dear, you do have to get better before you go home to Jonathan, don't you? That's why you're here. Now won't you tell us how you've been feeling this week? The group is here to help you, Mrs. Renshaw."

Renshaw might stop for a minute and look kinda worried, and Cobb sits up straight and waits like she's got somethin' good comin', but Renshaw's face starts smilin' again – that far-away smile – and then Cobb knows she's done for.

"It is frightfully difficult to find good help these days, isn't it, darling?" Renshaw says. "There is always some dreadfully embarrassing mistake in the table-setting, isn't there, darling?"

Cobb gives it up and turns to Mrs. Bloom. She can count on old Ida Bloom for some sad story to hang onto. Bloom's old man died a year ago, and the old lady can't forget him. He must o' been some kinda lover, that husband o' hers; old Ida's over sixty, and she just can't forget the dude.

"Oi." Mrs. Bloom says, "how it's going by me, you ask? Stones on the heart, Nurse. My Simon's dead, this is by me hard to believe. Simon was my life. Without him, what's to feel, I ask you?"

"And what about your children, Mrs. Bloom?" Cobb asks.

"Children? Sure, God bless them, I have my children, knock wood. But what comes from children? They have by them a life, they have their own children, knock wood.

"My Simon was by me a friend, oi, a king he was. Every Shabbos, a box of chocolates he would bring, a beautiful bouquet from flowers. T'would come a holiday. Rosh Hashanah, right away Simon would bring me a beautiful dress, special. We would talk together hand-in-hand." Old Bloom starts cryin' round about then. "Oi, a king died by me, it's already dead by me the heart. I'm telling you the truth, Nurse, every night I dream from Simon. Oi, I wish already I should be with him in the other world, Nurse. Here is already finished . . ." And so on.

Cobb gets a little tired of hearin' Mrs. Bloom soundin' the

sometimes, she looks like she's tired o' listenin' to the same record – but she needs Mrs. Bloom to keep things rollin' in here. Mrs. Bloom's the only one makes any kinda sense, and gives Cobb somethin' to get her teeth into in these here groups. Her and me and Dana. We're the only ones give Miss Cobb a handle in these here meetings. We keep the music goin' for her. Without us, there wouldn't be no meetin' at all; she'd be like a drummer without no drum.

Like Mr. Archer, the cat I share my room with. He's a clean enough dude – not all raggedy-lookin' like Eddy – an' real smart – the guy used to be a teacher or somethin' – but he don't speak the same language as anyone else. Archer's polite as all hell, and good lookin', an' his voice is real deep and classy – but he says everything in them poetry rhymes. Ya can't get a straight answer outta him.

> To be or not to be.
> That is the question,
> Whether 'tis nobler . . .

That's how Archer starts.

"You're depressed, Mr. Archer," Cobb says in a sweat. "Is that what you're trying to tell us? Could you tell us about it in your own words, Mr. Archer, without quoting poetry? We'd like to help you, Mr. Archer."

Cobb can't go nowhere with him. She'd have to be some big college professor to know what the dude's talkin' about, that's what I think, and anyway the cat don't give her no kinda satisfaction.

It's Mrs. Bloom Cobb turns to for the heavy stuff. She says Bloom ain't facin' reality, and isn't it time she began to think of facin' her life without Simon?

"You must start living your own life, Mrs. Bloom," Cobb says.

"You must start living your own life, Mrs. Bloom," Cobb says.

Then maybe I'll tune in just to make Cobb feel good. "Yeah, Bloom Mama, how 'bout you call your sister and join that there ladies' club she goes to? Hey, that might be a cool club."

And Dana might say somethin' just to put Cobb on; Dana gets high puttin' her on. "Mrs. Bloom, like, why don't you take up knitting? My grandmother does that, and you know what? She sells her sweaters to all kinds of people, and she keeps busy, like."

Dana will turn to Eyes, lookin' like a real sweet 'n' steady little schoolgirl, and she'll say, "Don't you think that's a good idea, like, Miss Cobb? You always say we have to have healthy hobbies, like, Miss Cobb."

You never can tell for sure if Miss Cobb thinks we're puttin' her on, but sometimes I think she knows, and she's madder 'n hell about it. She kinda moves her head in that tight regular way that says she's the boss. She smiles a little – not a real-heart smile – one o' her uppity half-smiles like she's tellin' us we're the ones crazy, not her. She closes her eyes like she's real satisfied. Pulls together all her folders 'n' papers, stands up real tall, reminds us to pull the chairs back into place, and thanks us for sharing our experiences today."

Me and Dana always end up bustin' our guts laughin' after she's gone, 'cause there ain't nothin' comin' down in these meetin's. Ain't nothin' happenin' ever. Just Mrs. Bloom tellin' her story, and me and Dana pretendin' we're into believin' there's somethin' happenin' here that's gonna help us, and old Miss Cobb listenin' to all that bullshit about tellin' the truth and sharin' feelin's.

It's always like that, gives me and Dana a laugh, and makes me feel good I haven't lost my touch. Until today, when Miss Cobb comes into our t-group, wearin' a cool-lookin' purple dress with some kinda black belt tied around her waist instead o' that white uniform she always wears. High-heeled shoes too with some fancy strap around the ankle.

I ain't seen Miss Cobb like any kinda woman before. I mean, I know she's not a man, but I don't think o' her in no-kind o' woman way either. She's about forty-five, for one, and I'm twenty-eight, and besides she wears that straight white nurse's uniform and carries that clip-board and that medicine tray that makes her look like some kinda walkin' machine with no regular woman-curves showin' at all. She never laughs like a woman does, and she never shows any real leg to speak of – just a tiny bit o' thick-stocking space between her starched dress and her white laced shoes.

I always think o' Cobb as part o' these walls, closed in here like we are except maybe she goes home nights. I never even think o' Miss Cobb goin' to sleep nights, maybe gettin' into somethin' soft that shows off a woman's breasts and hangs onto a bit o' thick woman-hip and clings to a woman's bottom like a curtain.

It throws me right off when I see Miss Cobb today – her waist closed in with that leather belt like it's beggin' to be opened, and the leg she's showin' just from the knee down with some soft sweet thigh peekin' out when she crosses one over the other. It near about blows my mind, and when Dana asks her in a scared voice that sounds like she's gonna cry or somethin' why she's wearin' that there dress, I just put my eyes down like I'm cooled out and not listenin' at all, but my ears tune in hot 'n' heavy.

When Cobb tells her it's hospital policy now that staff

should be wearin' street clothes, so the patients can feel freer to "express" themselves, I get busy tyin' up my right sneaker laces, and whistle inside my head, and say to myself, "Shee-it!!"

Just about then, Cobb asks me her usual question: "Now how are you fee-ee-ling today, Jerome?"

I just can't come up with any o' the easy bull I usually shoot. I feel my ears gettin' hot and my hands gettin' kinda wet, and I just keep my head down and keep noddin' like some real lame wimp, and can't say nothin' at all.

Dana has the same trouble, only different from mine. She can't stop talkin', and it ain't like she's puttin' Cobb on for fun like always. She can't keep her mouth shut. The words just keep runnin' away, and every second word is about the goddamned dress, like it's the most important thing in her life.

"What size dress is that, Miss Cobb?" Dana says in a real nervous voice. "I mean, it's not my business, but you're not as small as me, are you? I mean, I wear a size three. I mean, you should see me when I'm dressed up, I look beautiful and everything. You don't think I'm getting fat, do you? I like to dress up and go out sometimes. I'm stuck in here, I never get to go out and dress up like, I've got a real pretty purple dress at home – it's only a size three – I bought it in the junior department."

Poor Dana starts to cry, and she don't have nothin' to wipe her nose with. She's sittin' right beside me and snifflin', wipin' her nose with her knuckles, hands so skinny you can see all those ugly blue veins stickin' out.

"I can't win," she says. "If I eat, I get so fat, they all laugh at me. And then, if I don't eat, they put me in a hospital, and say I'm crazy. I'm never right. I want to get out of here." She pushes her coffee cup off the side of her chair. It smashes on the floor, and the coffee puddle just sits there lookin' like some stale brown piss, and nobody moves.

Miss Cobb nods a little, and says, "Go ahead, Dana. Tell us what you're feeling."

Mrs. Bloom comes in, with her goddamned old-lady's voice dronin' on and on about her goddamned Simon. Her voice goes loud after a while: "In a crazy house yet I'm sitting, Nurse!"

Eddy gets up in his corner, and starts hollerin' "crazy-house, crazy-house, crazy-house" over and over again like he can't get himself unstuck.

I just keep lookin' down at my sneakers tryin' to keep my head clear, tryin' to keep myself from thinkin' all those thoughts I'm thinkin'. Thinkin' about all the women out there on those streets I never get to seein'. All the music inside o' me dyin' and turnin' to shit. All the good gigs I'm missin' while I'm locked up here in this loony bin. All those guys out there, hot and cookin', makin' some real fine music like I used to, standin' up there an' jammin' an' hearin' those people clap 'n shout. Pullin' in those bucks and pullin' together that sound. Makin' hot love to some real fine fox right after a gig, gettin' on top of her and holdin' her close in the night, feelin' her warm and wet inside, feelin' her reach up strong and steady inside me, tastin' her mouth all hungry for more, hearin' her voice come slow 'n' easy, soft warm woman-voice climbin' up louder, better, fingernails bitin' into my back, sweet sound climbin' up to a howl –

"Jerome!" Cobb is lookin' at me. "Eyes" herself – woman-eyes, with that damn purple thing on, and her legs crossed at the knees makin' me blind. "You haven't said very much today, Jerome. Do you have something to add to our discussion?"

I can't get hold o' my voice, it's stuck somewhere inside

me mixed with all that heavy slimy stuff buildin' up in my throat. I can't say nothin'.

Till Archer comes on in my head, old Archer with his radio voice and one o' his lame-assed poetry lines. "Tears, idle tears . . ."

Before I know it, I'm at him, hittin' him square in the jaw with a left, gettin' him smack in the nose with a right, and the orderlies are at me, four of 'em, pinnin' my arms behind my back.

Before they drag me out, to hit me with one o' those big motherfucker needles that knocks people clean out, I spot old Cobb. She looks kinda pleased with herself, gatherin' her folders together, pickin' up her clip-board, switchin' her hips real pretty. Switchin' her hips from side to side, back and forth, just like a real foxy woman on the block after she's gotten her man to give her exactly what it is she wanted.

THE HELPER

Over the years Rustner spent working for the agency, he had developed a habit of sucking his gums, partly, it seemed, to relieve some unidentified hurt in them and partly to enable him to think more clearly. He thought constantly. He thought about his work, about his wife, his father, and he thought about the boys he went to high school with, the boys who had become scholars, lawyers, and accomplished businessmen. On Monday morning, Rustner was particularly thoughtful and depressed. He sat in his tiny office and brooded.

There were hurts for Rustner to bear. Just yesterday, he had gone to the bakery for his Sunday treat of bagels, cottage cheese and a little of that rich cheese cake with strawberry topping that soothed his gums. He was feeling good. His wife, Sheila, was with him, and she had dressed for him. True, her beige linen skirt was tight around the stomach, and consequently a little shorter in the front than it was in the back, but he had urged her to put on a girdle, and with the girdle and her black vinyl purse, she looked quite smart. She had the well-groomed appearance of the other wives he saw at the bakery on Sundays, those confident women who pointed out their food selections carelessly with polished finger-nails and glittering rings and dangling bracelets. Sheila looked almost like one of them, he thought, less expensive, but passable.

Rustner was wearing his favourite casual-rich outfit, his good, freshly cleaned brown slacks and his new beige shirt, several buttons undone at the top, the way he had seen those unbuttoned, affluent men wear theirs. He was proud of

Sheila and of himself too – so proud that he remembered to suck his gums less frequently even though they ached a little.

But when he walked into the bakery, it was all ruined. The good proud feeling left him as soon as he spotted Senson, who had been such a nothing in high school, a shy, pale, poor boy with just average marks. There was Senson, standing near the pickled fish counter, one tanned arm around the waist of his wife, an exquisitely fashionable young woman with sleek black hair and a slender well-kept body. When had Senson developed those shoulders and that height? How did his wife manage to look so delicately young and rich? Rustner suddenly felt furious at Sheila's wide girdled hips, her humbled round shoulders, the crooked run in her stockings. He felt silly in his ridiculous open-collared shirt; his gums began to ache meanly.

Red-faced and panicky, he pulled Sheila quickly out of the bakery, afraid that Senson might see him and talk down to him. To hell with the creamy cheese cake, Rustner thought. He hustled Sheila across the busy street in front of the bakery and down the two blocks to their flat, opened a can of sardines, and ate them while he was standing, dripping sardine oil carelessly all over his new beige shirt.

Rustner, still smarting from yesterday's hurt, sat at his desk, waiting for Mr. Wiener to come for his ten o'clock appointment. Senson had opened up all the old sores. Rustner thought about his father, the way the old man slaved and worried all his life and died broke. He thought bitterly about the size of his office window – a pathetic little hole, hardly a window at all compared to the larger picture windows all the other workers had. He suffocated in this trap daily. He could imagine himself gazing significantly out of a larger office window as he talked to his clients with the wisdom of a real professional. For a second, Rustner felt better. He had, after all, studied for four years to become a professional social worker; it was a dignified and worthy title. And he had to admit that when things went really smoothly with a case, when he managed to efficiently iron out all the little problems and get prompt, tangible results, he felt pleased with himself.

Rustner sipped some coffee and relaxed a little. What did it matter, after all, if the others had gotten the bigger offices with dignified-looking rugs? Was it really important that he had somehow been relegated to the financial cases at the Family Welfare Agency and that the others had prestigious-sounding caseloads, their clients in need of therapy, supportive intervention, rather than simple financial assistance?

The next sip of coffee was sour; the word "therapy" always made him feel sour. The image of suntanned Senson flashed through his mind again. Senson had become a lawyer and gotten himself right up there with Robinson & Wright; Rustner had looked him up in the phone book last night to check. And where had he gotten in his agency? he asked himself. Nowhere – that was the awful persistent truth. He had never been assigned one pure therapy case; after ten years of diligent service in this agency the only work he was ever allowed to do was hand out money, arrange budgets, help yellow old men and tiring greedy women complete their requests for old-age pensions, disability pensions, family assistance, and every sort of supplementary assistance. How humiliating to be locked into this little box at the end of the corridor only to fill in slips of paper. How utterly shaming it was at staff meetings to hear Lane, the agency director, say without hesitation, "Mr. Rustner, you can go now. We're about to begin consultation with Dr. Rickdorf about the counselling and therapy cases. This doesn't really apply to you."

Rustner slammed his fist hard on the desk; the pile of yellow financial assistance sheets flew off. His gums hurt badly now; his yellow papers were all over the floor, and his hands were sweating.

Rustner's office door opened slowly. When he looked up, he saw Mr. Wiener walking in, carrying his cane in one hand, and at least five grubby envelopes in the other. Rustner watched him drop his body heavily into the chair closest to him and start to talk in a loud voice, high-pitched with anxiety: "Another letter, Rustner. Again a refusal. What should I do? I'm sixty-six already. I paid taxes all my life, didn't I?" Leaning forward, he pushed the most recent letter towards Rustner. Rustner waved his hands to silence Wiener. "Just hold on a minute, Wiener, okay?" He picked up the letter wearily and started to read. The old-age application form had been inadequately completed, the letter informed; details of Wiener's exact date of arrival in Canada some fifty years back had been inconsistent. The ship, Magentic, from which he had disembarked was not the same ship as had been reported earlier.

Rustner looked up at Wiener's flushed worried face, and pitied him. He remembered his own father's anxiety during the slow season in the clothing business, how he used to call the foreman three times a day to ask if maybe a little work would come in soon, perhaps a rush job from the contractor before the season picked up again. He remembered the way his old man would sweat and panic about rent day, pacing around the house, worrying, always worrying about what would happen if he was caught a few dollars short. His memories were interrupted by the sound of Wiener tapping his cane on the floor. Wiener impatiently stuttered: "This is your job, after all, Mr. Rustner. You help only with the pensions here."

Rustner leaned back slowly in his chair and smiled carefully. "No, Mr. Wiener, you're quite wrong there. It's your job, you see. It's your pension, isn't it now? I can help you to help yourself. You'll simply have to trace the name of that ship."

Wiener was coughing now, paling with helplessness. "Go home this evening and call your sister again. Ask her to look through her papers. The name of the ship must be listed accurately on one of them," Rustner told him.

"She doesn't know, I told you before. She looked." Wiener waved his hands vaguely, a frail gesture of hopelessness. Rustner reached for a pen, wrote a date on the Wiener folder, and started to file it in his desk drawer. "That's all, Mr. Wiener," he said, "my next client is waiting." Wiener shakily got up to go, drained of his earlier energy.

Later that evening Rustner remembered Wiener's raging cough and his wrinkled hands. He vowed that he would look after the Wiener case in the morning, write a letter to the Pension Board explaining the inadequacy of ship records available, and asking for immediate reconsideration of the case.

But the next morning, Wiener was in again, waiting for Rustner in the agency lobby when he arrived, hurrying him with his own anxiety, waving his wretched old cane. "Rustner, I couldn't find anything. My sister doesn't know. I'm up already since five in the morning. I can't sleep with these worries. I'll end up in a home yet, God forbid. You must do something, Rustner."

Rustner flushed a little at the sound of Wiener's loud voice, imagining the lifted eyebrows and contemptuous expressions of the other two workers who were just checking in at the front desk behind them in the otherwise silent lobby. Wiener was edging up to Rustner, tugging at his sleeve and talking right into his face. "Rustner, Rustner, do something. Be a mensch. This pension business will finish me. Without my own little roof I'll die. Call . . . right away. Write maybe a letter. You know how, make somewheres a connection."

Wiener's breath was stale. He had moved so close to Rustner that the spray of spit escaping from his mouth caught Rustner right in the eye. Rustner stiffened. He tried discreetly to wipe the spit from his eye. "You haven't an appointment, Mr. Wiener," he said.

"What difference, an appointment . . . A man can't sleep all night, needs yet an appointment?"

Rustner saw the two young workers at the water cooler looking up and watching him critically. No, he decided, I won't write that letter today, I can't be had that easily. He led Wiener swiftly into his office, just to avoid a public scene. He sat with him for five minutes, dismissing him curtly, advising him that he, Rustner, didn't perform magic. These things took time. A man had to work harder at what was important to him and Wiener would have to work harder at finding the name of his ship.

At the staff meeting the next day, Rustner watched the heavy immigrant woman's breasts as she spoke. They were large and hard-looking breasts, and she folded her arms around them every time she finished making a point. Everyone seemed to be watching her with admiration, listening to her case review with awe, and afterwards, they asked animated questions.

"Helga, how did you manage to overcome the client's initial resistance?" one worker asked. "You did a marvellous job."

Helga spoke slowly and carefully, confident enough to take her time.

"I'm particularly interested in the way you used transference techniques here. Could you elaborate on this?" another asked.

Helga spoke again, joking a little, certain of being right about her technique. She had been in this country for only ten years and had become very well-known in that short time.

Rustner raged at the respect she inspired; he sat quietly in a corner, cursing those breasts. When they served coffee after the meeting, he left in a hurry. He didn't want coffee; he wouldn't have known which group to sit with anyway.

After lunch, he met with Mr. Marks, Mrs. Abrams, Mr. Sawchuk, and Miss Smith. Marks needed a hearing aid, and welfare didn't cover that; he had to have an official request. Abrams had to have taxi tickets; her back problem had gotten worse, and she just couldn't manage the buses on her own anymore. Sawchuk had taken his four kids and the wife out for a meal and a movie – his crippled boy's fourteenth birthday – and now he didn't have quite enough for the rent. And Miss Smith had just spent eighty dollars for the year's water tax, and she needed a supplement. She had been eating peanut butter and those cheap noodles for two weeks now; she was bloated, constipated and depressed – and her supply of noodles was running out.

Rustner worked at their forms quickly and furiously, avoiding their faces, unable to block out the image of Helga's bold breasts and her large confident voice.

By the time Wiener arrived at four, Rustner was tired and hungry. Today Wiener looked paler and smaller than usual, a frightened little man. His voice was somehow quieter and less demanding while he explained his landlord's threat. Wiener was two months behind in his rent, and the landlord wanted his money now. He could pay him, Wiener admitted, with the one hundred dollars he had in the bank and the forty dollars his sister would lend him, but what about next month? Ah, if his poor wife were alive; she would speak better than he. His wife had had a voice for landlords.

Rustner watched Wiener's eyes glisten as he told of his wife's courage with the fat boisterous landlord on Clark Street, the one who had put their furniture out on the street. Despite himself he was engrossed in Wiener's passionate description of his wife Leah running right up to the fat man and hurling insults at him, shaming the landlord into embarrassed retreat.

He saw Wiener nodding his head sadly and clearly heard his frail voice quavering as he finished his tale of Leah's triumph. "Oh, but Rustner," Wiener murmured, "this landlord, mine, is a different story. He's skinny and educated, and he talks quiet-like, slow. He told me yesterday he can't give me free rent . . . maybe I would be better in a rest home, he says. He cuts my throat when he says that . . . a home would right away kill me. Leah – may she rest in peace – can't help me now."

Rustner felt sorry for Wiener, remembering his own father's constant terror of landlords, the way he always worried about the roof over his head. God, Rustner thought, can I ever get away from this? First my skinny, frightened father and now Wiener. Why couldn't I have a father with a big cigar, who would send me to medical school or set me up in business? Always nothing but that skinny fear . . . No wonder I'm here, no wonder I'm nothing here. He pictured Helga's big strong breasts, and he suddenly hated Wiener and his snivelling fear. "Okay, Mr. Wiener, our time is up for today," he said. "Look again for your papers. We'll meet on Friday."

"But, Mr. Rustner, if I don't get my pension cheque I'm finished next month . . . no bed, no mattress. If you take away my roof, you kill me, Rustner."

Wiener's pleading frightened voice again reminded Rustner of his father's lifelong helplessness. He had been relieved when his father finally died and left him alone.

"We'll meet on Friday, Mr. Wiener," he said. "Remember I can't do your work for you." Go to hell, he thought.

When Rustner tried to make love to his wife that night, something choked him again. Sheila lay there, passive and reticent. He thought of the way she served his supper, of the way she served his bed – unenthusiastically, but with a poor wife's sense of duty to her breadwinner, to her husband, he thought, who kept a roof over her head. Not the professional – just the breadwinner. He clutched at her thin breasts frantically, urging fantasies of Rustner the Landlord, but he felt no power. He fumbled furiously with her silent hips, but no life came. Instead, Helga's confident breasts and his father's skinny fear. He looked at Sheila's face for some sign of eagerness or at least disappointment at his impotence; instead he saw only her flat mute expression of humble acceptance, maybe even relief. He wanted to smack her face, to rouse her somehow into some form of shocked aggression. He went to the kitchen, made himself a cup of tea, and thought of Wiener. Let the old bastard squirm, he thought.

On Friday, Wiener didn't show up for his appointment on time. He came a half hour late, slower and much calmer than usual, saying little, except that he hadn't found anything that would help. Rustner said he would write a letter to the authorities, but Wiener sat still. "I could help with this letter," Rustner repeated, but Wiener only nodded with exhausted resignation.

"Ah, Rustner," Wiener said weakly, "what can you do? Maybe you could help, maybe not. You're a hard worker, but a worker, a simple man, like me . . . Would they even listen to you?"

Rustner sat still awhile, looked at Wiener, said nothing, looked away. "Who knows?" Wiener repeated weakly, "The bosses . . . do they listen to people like us?"

Rustner's stomach tightened and his gums jabbed at him cruelly. "My feeling, Mr. Wiener, is that you don't really want to help yourself."

"Rustner!" Wiener broke in angrily, "What do I ask? Such a big job you have here? Such a big job to help an old man which he can't so much help himself?"

Rustner cleared his throat and spoke in his calmest professional voice. "Perhaps, Mr. Wiener . . . perhaps you would be happiest in a home for the aged, just as your landlord suggested."

He was going to continue when Wiener, his eyes brimming with tears, suddenly looked up and steadily stared at him. He kept his eyes fixed on Rustner's face as though, in the midst of his grief, he had been stopped by the recognition of something there, a piece of a puzzle, an answer to a mystery.

"Why, Rustner?" he asked. "Why? What makes a man like you should be so mean? What dybbuk makes you should stick a knife around and around in me on purpose?"

Rustner was bewildered by Wiener's question, frightened by the conviction in Wiener's wet eyes. He felt wretchedly cold and brutal. He could see Wiener's face growing steadily paler, his hands beginning to tremble convulsively, his body seeming to dwindle as he sat there, hunched over now. He wanted to reach out to comfort Wiener, to touch the old ugly wrinkled hand, but his own hands felt monstrously heavy, defiantly limp and weak, and his aching gums kept tearing at him, filling him with the distinct taste of blood.

FLYING ON OTHER VOICES

It's the red-headed kid in the metro station standing near the Laura Secord window salivating over the chocolates, he's the one warns me. Kid maybe twenty or twenty-one, Jeremy's age now. Skinny at the shoulders, freckles round his nose, pock marks on his chin, speaking out the side of his mouth.

"Cop upstairs the size of a bull," kid says. "Looking to bust ass. You'd best pull your shopping bags together, lady, and get out of here. Cold as hell out there, though."

My cough is so bad, it sounds like broken gravel, and the hurt in my chest is a damned ice-pick by now, but it's not the cough or the cold sent me underground today. Only one thing made me get off the streets today. It's those cats in the alley going crazy, screaming and fussing. That cat sound always drives me inside for cover.

"Push down the bottle of wine," the kid adds. "That's a sure giveaway. He'll bust you for sure unless you push that under."

It's strangers like him tell me the things I need to remember. I can count on their voices telling me. Garbage collectors sometimes tip me off there's half a Big Mac and fries in the bin, and I gotta dig deep to bring it up. Bus driver one time tells me to hop on the bus and move to the back and just sit there to keep warm. Warns me to push the empties far down in my bag so it looks normal. Strangers like these tell me what's safe to bring up, what needs bringing up, and what's the stuff needs pushing down and hiding.

Like feeding Jeremy all those years ago when he was

little. There was times I'd overdone it, and I needed to let him bring it up. And other times I needed to get that food down his throat, or he'd near about starve to death. It needed me to force his mouth open sometimes and push the food down, cruel as it was. Otherwise, he'd go for days without vegetables or meat in his system.

Oh, I could be mean when I got the panic in me. I'd pinch his nose and let him holler, and I'd force the food down. Never mind what the neighbours thought; I didn't care what the other women said. I knew they yakked about the kind of mother I was, so fixed on Jeremy, I wouldn't let him go to the corner store himself, even when he was seven and could get there without crossing a road.

I don't know what it was made me so scared to let the kid be. Could be it was his almost choking on my cord like he did in the first place. That's maybe what made me hold him tight like I did. Like letting go of him would open him up to every kind of evil. Like the angel of death that had almost had him at birth would catch up to him and not let him off this time. Not the second time round.

Bad luck got me the second time round, that's certain. I think of my marriage to Frank as two times round. It was Frank both times, but it was a different Frank each time, and the second time round was a death.

The first time round, me and Frank lived it up. Saturday night parties and lots of restaurants and high-stepping together. The whole nine yards. We had regular friends then. My cousin Tippie and her man, my best friend Ella and her hubbie, our next door neighbours Si and Louise. We did everything in couples, and Frank never looked at another woman without telling me I was the finer by far, the better dancer, the one with the best woman-shape, the one with the firmest-looking neck and arms.

We'd go out dancing dressed to the nines, Frank with his shirt collar starched just so and his black patent shoes gleamed to a shine. Me in full-skirted dresses, tight-waisted and low at the neck, with my breasts showing big like Frank liked them.

Four years of courting, it turned out to be, and two of them marriage years, and all that time Frank treated me so good, it wasn't like we were an ordinary married couple at all. It just turned into one long sweetheart dance, me leaning against Frank in the dance hall, and Frank guiding me round by the waist. I was his perfect China doll, he told me.

I think of those times often enough when I catch myself in the mirror, and see my face looking weather-lined like a fishwife's, and me all covered up, so there's no skin showing at all. Summer and winter, I'm covered in the same layers of rags, three layers of sweaters on top of each other and Frank's old nylon windbreaker on top of that to keep the damp wind from gutting too mean into my bones.

On bad days, when I dig into the trash can for something to fill me up, I think of the swell food we left behind on plates and what a feast those leftovers would make for scavengers like me. We always seemed to be eating. Barbecued chicken and ribs rich with gravy. Finger foods like chicken wings and deep-fried fish sticks and asparagus in butter and crispy potato skins. Little tiny meatballs on toothpicks. Frank would put pieces of food into my mouth and watch me chew and tell me how nice I was, and sometimes lick my fingers one at a time just to make me laugh.

Darned crazy how I remember every little thing Frank said that made me feel good, and every little thing around that too. Like cousin Tippie one night when she had all of us over to play cards, and she served take-outs from the deli and couldn't help showing off. She put out mushroom caps and little wieners in blankets and liver dip. She cooed about her dishes like they were her babies or something.

I didn't like the liver dip she served and told her so, and she held her nose up in the air, and sniffed and corrected me.

"Foie gras," she said.

"Same thing," I retorted. "It's liver, ain't it?"

"The livers of fatted geese," Tippie said, as though that made all the difference. "It's costly, I'll tell you."

"They force-feed those damned geese," Frank said to Tippie in his stand-up-for-me voice. "They force those geese, so you can get fat on it."

He squeezed my shoulder tight and said I was the smartest girl in the whole world.

I stopped being his pretty smart girl as soon as I started carrying Jeremy though, in my fifth year of marriage. When my stomach first turned big, Frank's eyes narrowed.

"Your legs look like toothpicks with your stomach swelled," he said to me one day. "Awful sight, that is."

By the seventh month, I was so huge, I started having trouble catching my breath, and Frank's face went a dough-paste colour, and his mouth turned down, like he'd seen something mighty disgusting and he was madder than hell about it. Sometimes he'd try to make a joke for me and he'd force a laugh, but it never came out right, no kind of way.

He couldn't do much in bed anymore, either. It frightened me the way he'd push down on my head and expect me to fix things. He'd go soft on me each time he tried, and pulling on him made me think of blood sausages, plump and limp and nauseating to the taste. But I'd manage to push him into fullness eventually, and Frank would always say the same thing. "It's come to life," he'd say, surprise in his voice, as though his parts didn't belong to him at all.

"Get a move on!" It's the bull cop talking to me, now that I'm out on the street. "No sitting here on the sidewalk like dead-weight," he says.

I know better than to argue with this one, even though the vent I'm sitting against is a good one, air streaming out so steady, it feels like a kitchen stove. I gather my bags and pull myself up to standing, and try to ignore the bull's voice.

"Get some life in you," he shouts, and he kicks one of my bags. "Move it!"

When Jeremy got the headache in him, I gave him aspirin and forced some juice into him, but after he vomited, I let him be. Then the fever came high, and he had a rash on his back and couldn't get out of his bed at all. Frank started bullying him something awful.

"I want him dressed and out of that bed," Frank said. "I won't have no son of mine laying in bed all day like a sissy."

"For Jesus' sake, Frank," I said. "He's only a little thing of eight, and he's got such a heat inside him."

"It's old maids lie round in bed with a fever all day," Frank said. "No son of mine. Up!" he said to Jeremy. "Out of bed. Get a move on."

Little Jeremy pulled himself up onto his elbows, and looked into Frank's face. He blinked a few times, and then he started crying. He bawled with his mouth wide open and his head thrown back, and Frank grabbed his arm and started to yank him out of bed.

I stepped in. I spoke up, even though I knew how mad it would make Frank.

"Get off of him," I yelled.

Frank turned around to glare at me, his eyes fire-mad. "Who the hell you think you're talking to?" he shouted.

"I won't have you bullying him, "I screamed. "Keep your hands off him!"

"Why, you . . ." Frank held a fist up in the air and spit on the rug in Jeremy's room. Big gob of spit on the rug, just as though he were some kind of vagrant coughing up his phlegm at curbside, never knowing any home at all.

I remember thinking Jeremy's rash was spreading and he seemed to be getting hotter, and I called the doctor and begged him to come. I remember the doctor saying it was a bad flu Jeremy had, and telling me to keep up the aspirin and fluids and telling me not to worry myself into the ground. I remember Jeremy swallowing his pills that afternoon without making no kind of fuss and then falling asleep kind of heavy, drooling over the blue pillow. Late in the night, Jeremy's face was hotter than it had been all day and I heard rasping noises in his chest the sound of something hard breaking and, then, it was me calling the hospital and ordering an ambulance and telling them never mind the expense of it.

Later that night in hospital, there's the sound of me making gagging noises with my mouth wide open and no scream coming out at all. I remember thinking how ugly I must look for all the world to see, with my tonsils showing, and people around me looking, and no kind of shame in me at all. I remember thinking there's a huge black hole in the sky, and God has fallen through.

What happened in between the afternoon when Frank grabbed Jeremy's arm and the big black hole of night, I don't know. I couldn't never connect the two. Like some kind of horror picture when one scene changes into something completely different, and you never see how one thing gave way to the next.

The coughing in me starts up now, rises harder and harder till it feels like something is going to tear inside of me. Fits of coughing pull at my insides, something fierce, like the labour pains when I was pushing Jeremy out. I need something to stop the hurt, but there's no one beside me to help at all. Only slushy sidewalks with snow muddied and mean, and not even a stranger beside me to take my side. I'll have to take care of the hurt my own way, carry my own self to hospital without asking anyone else.

I changed my mind about the ambulance. I called back and cancelled. I couldn't trust them to do it. They'd be rough with Jeremy, that's what I decided. They wouldn't know what a mother knows about carrying.

The cab took too long to come, and I ended up carrying Jeremy the two blocks to hospital instead. He lay limp and quiet all the way, the weight of him heavier than I'd remembered him to be, like he was a new child in my arms and not my firstborn at all. He lay in my arms and never said a word, but his breathing was loud.

I passed an alley, and the yowling of cats rushed out at me. It was a sad scary noise, and I remembered right then what Ma used to say about cats' screaming. "Awful bad omen, that. Turn a shoe over," she used to say, "so the bad luck will be turned around."

I started running when I heard the cats. "Feral cats," Ma used to say, "ugly things." I ran and ran and got in here, with my baby awful quiet and heavy as stone in my arms.

Place full of crazies is what this is. Same thing as always. Place for the sick pulls in the crazies. The crazies and the tramps.

Tramps come in here to get out of the cold. Crazies come in to cry their hearts out. Seats lined up all along the wall outside the emergency, people sitting here with their legs sprawled out in front of them and their galoshes dripping snow and wet. Some of them holding their heads in their hands like they're in mourning or some awful thing and waiting for someone to come and save them.

Crazies on all sides of me, laughing one minute and cussing the next. Talking to themselves to beat the band.

Two-way conversation going on right beside me here. Young fellow looking like an everyday kind of man with a house and a family and things that belong to him, ordinary fellow like that, starts a conversation all of a sudden, you'd think there's twelve people built themselves a house between his ears. I can't help listening. Fella's got so many voices coming out of his mouth, you'd think he needs a conductor to keep them straight. He's wild crazy, this one is. Squeaking with a little girl's voice one minute, answering with a soldier's voice the next, hollering at his mama, cursing her out and wishing her dead, you'd think she'd tried to poison him or something.

When he starts telling his daddy how he's going to crush his bones in a blender and drink him whole, I remember I'm supposed to be scared of anyone going off his head like this one. And then I remember I'm not scared. Not of him. Not at all.

Only one thing scares the living daylights out of me. It's my little boy, Jeremy; they've got him right there in the quiet room, and I haven't seen hide nor hair of him ever since I brought him into this place and they snatched him out of my arms. Scooped him up like he didn't belong to me, and ran with him into that green-walled room where they mean to have him to themselves. They won't let me in. I've knocked three times, and each time they've turned me away.

I haven't made a fuss. Not yet. I'm holding on to it, waiting for them to open that door and let my baby run back to me. I'm biding my time, is what. It wouldn't do to make a stink. Not in a place like this. They're the bosses here, them in their white coats and choking instruments hung around their necks. Better to zip my lip and wait until they're ready to give him back. They'll fix him for me, he's mine, it's a pill I need from them to make my Jeremy well again. But he's mine; they can't keep him.

The bone-crusher next to me is getting himself into a fury now. Got his knickers in a knot, like Frank used to say. He's standing up and talking to Jesus in a voice sounds like thunder. He's challenging Jesus to a fist fight right here. All the people on the vinyl chairs are moving away real-quiet-like, moving down the row, like they got something to see further down the aisle. Faces sneaky and all closed up, so the Jesus-fighting bone-crusher doesn't take any notice of their moving and whip their noses out of shape before he turns them into meal.

I should be moving too, if I was one of them. If I was scared like everyone else round here, I'd move – but I'm not scared. Not today. Not now. Nothing can scare me. Nothing except Jeremy. Nothing matters until they let me get my boy back.

"Nothing! You hear that? No frigging Frank or doctor with your nose held high in the air telling me I waited too long, and taking him away. Get out of my face! Out of my face the whole frigging bunch of youse, and let me see him. Let me see him now! Now! Now!"

My ears sting. I cannot stand it, the trembling-shrieking-woman-voice mixing in with that other voice fighting the fight with Jesus. It shouldn't be allowed, all this shrieking – one crazy screaming louder than the next. They should put a stop to it. I mean to complain, but there's a strong hand on my lap stops me now, and a white-coated person looking close into my face, and then I realize the crazy woman-shriek is mine.

"Ma'am," she has her hand on my knee, and I slap her off.

"Let go of me. Give him back, harlot! He's mine. He came out of me, and you can't take him. In the name of God, you cannot have my boy!"

"Please, ma'am." Her voice is quiet, but she is not so scared now that she has two white coats behind her ready to wrestle with trouble. "You aren't allowed to loiter in these hallways, even though it's cold on a night like this. I'm truly sorry, but it's hospital policy."

"Loiter, me arse!" I croak at her. "You took him, and I want him back. You hear me?"

They have me in the green-walled room, the room they wouldn't let me enter last time round. They've done something to me. Whatever it was, it made me sleepy and quietened the shaking in me that had me screaming for Jeremy like it was God knows how many years ago, and he was still little and mine to hold. The thing that quietened my shaking makes me remember.

I know this much now. It's a long time later, and there's no way of getting that time back and no way of changing what can't be changed. I came into this awful place today because of the cough in me and the ice-pick hurt in my chest,

and something happened inside me, and I screamed the beje-
sus out of my lungs to bring back my Jeremy.

But Jeremy's not here. I know that now. I lie on the cot
where they've placed me, and look up at the little black holes
in the ceiling, and remember what's not mine to have.
Jeremy's not here. I had to let him go. There's not a goddamn
blessed thing I can do about it. It's only me now, me and my
cough and the ice-pick in my heart.

"My boy," I say.

"It's your cough we need to care for, Mrs. Arliss," the
young doctor says. "We want to keep this cough from turning
into pneumonia."

"I wouldn't care," I say out loud, "I wouldn't care a damn
if I died right this moment."

She looks at me, and sighs.

"It isn't easy to lose a child," she says. "I know that. It's
got to be the hardest thing in the whole world." She says it so
much like she means it, the tears come up hot in my eyes and
throat, and I can't say anything, except to lie here, and gulp
and swallow and remember the whole terrible all of it.

She touches my shoulder and pushes my hair back and
pulls the curtain snug around me and leaves me to my remembering. Remembering the part I couldn't remember before. I
look up at the ceiling and remember the black holes that came
into my eyes that day. Black so thick in my eyes I'm blind, like
someone's poked my eyes out so I won't have to go on seeing.
The cat sounds start up in my ears to tell me. Cat sounds so
mournful in my ears, I know Jeremy is in bad trouble.

I break into the quiet green room, push against the nurse
holding me back, and then I see. It is not quiet at all. Everyone
pouncing on Jeremy. Eight or nine of them doing awful
things to my Jeremy, pushing pipes into his throat, trying to
cut his throat open.

He's such a good boy, he doesn't say a word. He lets them attack him, and he doesn't let go a cry. I won't let them. They aim to take his head off, but I'm here to stop them. I scratch with my nails, and bite and kick and will not let them. They pin me down and stick something in me, and when I woke, he was dead. My little boy was dead.

It didn't help to know it was meningitis killed him, and it happened too fast, and they tried everything. It didn't help to know they weren't cutting his head off at all, but doing a tracheotomy instead to save him. It did no good to know that everyone on staff worked on him and neglected everyone else in emergency that night. It had all come to nothing.

They put me up on the nut ward afterward. They let me walk the corridors all day, back and forth, counting the square tiles underneath.

I never got to the funeral. While I was counting the tiles underfoot, Frank sold the house behind me. While they had me in hospital, he got rid of everything – and it was gone, all of a sudden. Gone as though it had never been – Jeremy and Frank and the house all together.

I came out of the hospital onto the street with my clothes in two shopping bags, and a light gaberdine coat on my back, and that's where I stayed. I slept the first night in a passage-way with my head on a stair, and woke up in the morning, and took to the streets again.

It was where I wanted to be. I didn't have a home any-more. I didn't want to go home.

Out on the streets with strangers whispering warnings and messages to me and walking away into the night, I knew I had a chance. I could catch a peek of someone moving along the sidewalk, looking just like Jeremy for a flash of a second, and then moving on. I could catch a sound. There could be a voice drifting through the night air lifts me up and makes me believe I hear him. Voice like Jeremy's coming close, close to my ear, and then fading, like a stranger who knows me and cares for me and whispers things to me, but has to keep on moving.

WINDOWS

It is always someone watching, and she the one not seeing. They ask her the same question over and over again. She knows there's a bunch of them on the other side of the glass, listening for the answer.

Questions like a riddle: "What is the worst thing you can remember? The best, then? What is the best?" All of them watching her face from the other side to see where it cracks, to see the words spilling out of her mouth like broken teeth.

What is the worst thing you can remember, they ask, and she lowers her eyes and looks like she is trying to look back to then.

She is trying, but there are windows made of thick ribbed glass in her way that will not let her see. She can look, but she cannot see. Everything on the other side is blurred because of the thickness of the glass, like the steam that rose from the sidewalk in the heaviness of August. Waves of heat rose from the sidewalk in the summer, thick as syrup.

Dust on Ma's window too, sticky film of dust that stuck to her cheeks when she pressed her nose hard against the window-pane, trying to see through to the street below. Always the thick windows that did not let you see.

Nobody could see in that house. Summer and winter, everyone inside stayed groggy like drunk people. Ma saw nothing, with Pa gone and Him in the house regular, giving her money and talking snarly about Pa. Uncle Big with his Austrian accent, mustache curled at the tips, hands large and white. Hands too clean, nails sharpened and polished to a plastic sheen.

Like the hands of the dentist at the clinic where she went to get her first tooth pulled. She waited in the hallway with Ma for more than an hour that time. A long line of people in the hallway, and nobody saying anything. Only sitting on the hard wooden chairs with their hands folded in their laps.

She could see the dentist's shadow behind the glass, but nothing clearer than that. Bumpy thick glass window on the dentist's door. She waited in the hallway for longer than an hour, medicine-stink in her nose – that and the scared-sweat stink of the others waiting.

The dentist started to pull her back tooth with just a jab of freezing, hardly enough to take away the hurt, but she could not tell him that she was not ready. She winced, but she did not dare say he had not given her enough. He was a dentist, after all, tall and white-haired with medicine-smelling hands. Hands smelling harsh and too clean, doctor-clean, making Ma's voice sound scared when she talked to him. She did not say the dentist had not waited long enough for the freezing to take hold, because Ma could not pay; the clinic was free to those who could not pay.

Ma took her out for a coke afterwards at a little place with a counter and stools to sit on. Coke in a thick green-tinted bottle. The man behind the counter looked down his nose at her and said, "You shouldn't be drinking that all by yourself, girl! You should be sharing that with your mama. Children these days got no concern." He made his eyes into narrow mean slits like Uncle Big's eyes when he wanted her to be still.

Ma said, "That's okay. Poor child just had her tooth pulled." The man looked sour and said nothing more, and she could feel her face turning red. She looked down at her shoes, shame burning hot inside like a fiery thing in her stomach.

When the dentist started yanking, she pushed at his wrist, she could not help it. He stopped for only a minute. He looked at Ma and said, "If you don't hold her hands down tight, you will not come back to this clinic ever again. Do you hear me?"

She did not push the dentist's wrists after that – she felt Ma's hands clammy around hers. She tried to help Ma hold her. She held herself tight and all frozen inside that chair, she made her head go far far away, to the quiet place where there was lots of grass and small pebbles and water, and nobody could hurt her.

Afterwards, there was cotton stuffed into the hole where the tooth had been, and she pulled at the coke straw slowly from the other side of her face. Later, there would be cotton stuffed in her underwear to keep the blood from running down her leg, and Uncle Big would say that she ought to be careful now. She was big enough to do dirty things and he better not catch her, she had better not be caught. He did not want to hear about her carrying on like a whore with boys. Ever. There would be hell to pay; she would have to answer to him from now on.

At the restaurant counter, she asked Ma could they telephone Caroline to meet them now that it was over, and Ma said no. Caroline was keeping Uncle Big company at home, Ma said. They would tell Caroline everything when they got home.

"Did it hurt?" Caroline's eyes were red, she had been crying. She was blubbering, and eating the cruller they had brought home for her.

Cindy answered.

"No, no, it didn't hurt, not even a little bit!" It was better to say no to Caroline. When something bad happened,

Caroline would lie down on the floor and bang her head so hard, you would have to put a stick in her mouth to stop her from biting her tongue off. You had to be careful with Caroline. She had moods something wild, Uncle Big said that. Crazy-woman-fits, Uncle Big said.

"You ought to put her away," Uncle Big said. "Lock her up somewhere so's we can be safe. Girl this big has one of them cat fits, she could kill someone, she's got that much pounds on her. Solid blubber is what that is. That ain't no baby fat, I'm telling you that much. Don't kid yourself, just because she's yours. That girl could be a killer, she could turn on the whole bunch of us in the night. You never know when someone that loony-tunes could come at you with a kitchen knife."

At night, when Cindy goes down for a glass of water in the kitchen, she passes Caroline's room and she can see. She sees Uncle Big at the top of Caroline's bed, kneeling down beside her like he is praying. She can see him through the small crack in the doorway. He holds his mouth against Caroline's ear. She can see his hands moving under the blanket like humped animals running, looking for food.

He breathes loud, and moans sometimes like a man going under. Like a man drowning with his breath coming short and quick. Like he is trying to catch up with himself, and he cannot run fast enough.

"What are you seeing, Cindy?" This is what they ask her now. "When you look ahead like that into the air, what do you see?" They are hungry for her answer; they have pens and writing paper, and many of them wear white hospital coats.

She looks back to another window, the dusty window that looked from her bedroom down onto the street where Benjamin Stein used to sit on his doorstep after one of his crazy times. She can see him now. He does not move a muscle, his eyes do not blink. He sits on the stoop like a statue with his long hands held between his knees. The kids from the block have gathered around him. They yell into his face, to see if he will move. Benjamin Stein is a crazy man, Cindy knows that.

When he gets real crazy, he cannot move at all. His eyes go dead, and the ambulance men have to come to take him back there. To the mental hospital far away. They will lift him all in one frozen piece and place him on a stretcher wrapped round and round in white.

She knows it will happen even before it happens. She has seen it happen before when she was five maybe, or six. She leans her nose and face close up to the window and makes fog circles with her breath so she can peek. She wipes the fog circles with her fingers like peep-holes.

She knows all the bad parts that are coming because she has seen Benjamin Stein wild-eyed and crazy before this. She waits for the bad parts now.

"What do you see now, Cindy?" they ask. "When you stare straight ahead like that, what is there?"

She sees the window. She sees Benjamin Stein's eyes getting wide. Even though he cannot move – he has not moved for days, it is said; it is his condition, it is said – he goes red when he sees the two ambulance men coming towards him. He crouches all at once like he is gathering his strength and starts to run. He does not know where to push his body. He pivots on one foot, starts to go to one side, then he turns around to run the other way.

He cannot get past more than two houses. He is thrown to the ground, and fastened onto himself. His arms are pulled tight around him. He is lifted in one frozen piece onto the gurney, and pushed into the ambulance hole like a huge tray being slid into its place.

"Bagged," Uncle Big says afterwards. "Crazy as hell! They bag him like a goddamned piece of meat."

Uncle Big laughs. The laugh always comes out sounding mean. Mean like Cindy herself watching from the window all those times.

There is another window, but she cannot see it clear. She knows it is there, but it is covered with steam rising from the bathtub. When she takes a bath, the window disappears completely. She makes the water so hot, it almost scalds her skin. She lowers herself into the bath careful-slow.

Her body gets used to the pain of too-hot water. You can get used to any pain at all, she thinks, if you need to.

She needs the hot water to steam up the window. Small window near the top of the bathroom door. She can see it now, built into the door to let some light in.

He watched her through that window each time she took a bath. He said he was checking to see if she was scrubbing right.

She would run the water piping hot, so he would not see. Each time, she could hear him breathing hard outside the bathroom door. She could imagine him grinning and rising to his toes to look into the window.

The hot water steam would not let him see, but afterwards he would come to towel her dry, to check if she had washed the right way.

"Your uncle wants to help you towel up," Ma used to say. Ma used to close the door fast behind her, humming loud to herself.

"Don't think you can get away without scrubbing," he would say. "This is the way you're to do it," he would say. He ran the water hot all over again, so hot there was steam over the window. By the time the fog cleared from the window, it was over.

He ran his hands down the inside of her thighs. "Here," he said, "with the washcloth now. You do it like I showed you. Like this. Just like this."

He spread his fingers wide over her chest. "Dead upside-down birds, these titties," he said. "That is why they have died," he scolded, "because you let them get dirty. Lazy girl."

He said he would clean her so her insides would shine. He poked his lathered washcloth inside her. When she whimpered, he said she would soon be new. "Sparkling clean," he said. "Wait till your mama sees you. Your pa is no good," he said. "He has gone and left you. He is a good-for-nothing loser!"

By the time the fog cleared from the window and the bath water turned cold, she would try to slide down in it like she was drowning.

"Up!" he would say. "You must dry up now."

He wrapped her round and round in a huge towel each time. Tight tight wrap, like Benjamin Stein wrapped in white on the gurney. Then he brought her out to Ma. "She is all yours now," he would say. "Yeah. Now she is really clean like she ought to be."

"What makes you stare like this, Cindy?" they ask.

"What do you see when you stare?" She does not answer.

She knows how to keep her face perfectly still; nothing in it moves. She knows how to take her head away to a quiet place where there are pebbles and trees and water, and nobody can hurt her.

"The interview is over, Cindy," the nurse says to her, but

she is not ready to go. In her mind she has let herself into the nice quiet lake.

She slides down deep, down into the cooling waters. She lets her eyes close, lets the water rush into her nostrils. Her hair spreads out around her head, wet tentacles on the surface. She leans her neck back, feels the muscles of her neck relax.

"Ready, Cindy?" they ask. "Come on now. Ready, dear? The interview is over." They try to lead her out of the room by the wrists. They tug gently, one on each side.

When they start to pull at her wrists, she thinks of Uncle Big. The water is not pleasant anymore. Now, she is lying in the scummy bathwater instead. She sees Uncle Big in her mind and feels him tugging at her wrists. She fights against him. She screams and holds back, but he is stronger than she is. She cannot win this way.

She imagines herself a drowned girl instead. Frozen drowned girl with a grimace on her face. The grimace is almost a smile.

She imagines Uncle holding her high up in the air. He turns her round and round on all sides like a frozen fish. He turns her, inspecting her high in the air, close to the light coming in through the window.

WEEK-END

It had to rain. There had not been a summer like this since Oscar had been a kid back in the 1930s. The heat made his heart beat crazy hammer-leaps; the syrupy air made his eye-lids heavy. He ignored the discomfort as best he could, though the heat had made him short-tempered too. In the carwash this morning, the young attendant had forgotten to wipe down the chrome on his car – and Oscar had bellowed loud enough to make the manager come over.

The kid was probably damned hot too, he thought later. He should have remembered that. Why did he think that he was the only one whose throat was feeling like dried bark, and whose head was doing a dizzying set of turns on the top of his neck.

The vertigo was so bad now, he felt like lying down and forgetting about picking up Shawn and Samantha after all. He would not do it, though. Not for anything would he cancel this week-end with the kids.

It had been hard enough to get his daughter Jen to con-sent to his having them for the week-end. When he first suggested taking them to the cottage, she had paled and said "Well, maybe" in a strained voice that embarrassed him.

He let it go that time, but he brought it up again the night he took them all out to dinner. He had just spent sixty-eight bucks on Chinese food, and the kids were clamouring for ice-cream. He decided to use that moment to ask Jen again. She held back a minute, then looked over at Henry with the intimate-married-couple look which always made Oscar feel like a fifth wheel.

"Yeah, sure, Dad," she said in a nervous rush of breath. "Henry and I could go for that. Won't it be fun, children, going off to the nice country with Grandpa for the weekend?" The kids whooped with excitement, but he was not sure whether it was the ice cream coming up which made them so agreeable, or the trip itself.

It was a victory for him, nevertheless. The whole issue of his grandchildren had become a contest with Sandra. When he had left her and the kids years back, Sandra had been sliding backwards and he had been racing ahead. By the time the girls were in their teens, Sandra weighed over two hundred pounds and she rarely left the house. She kept her voice down when she talked, as though she did not want to be heard.

His business was thriving at the time, his body was lean and muscular, he was lunching with important people. He had learned to carry himself tall when he walked into a room.

Sandra refused to try. Each time he suggested losing weight or taking a course to get out of the house, she would lower her eyes and pretend not to hear. She had a way of closing him out. It was one of the reasons he had let himself fall for Selena when he did, he argued to himself. His wife had changed into someone else.

Now, the tables had turned. Sandra had slimmed down, changed her hairstyle, and she had become a successful real-estate agent. She had the house he left her, a promising man at her side, and a brand new car. The most painful part was that Sandra was still very close to their girls; she frequently had the grandchildren over to her house overnight.

He had nothing. When he had gone bankrupt, Selena had dumped him, and gotten every cent he had left. Here he was, a fellow of sixty with little money and plenty of debt, living in a budget apartment with only the ratty basement furniture which Selena had left behind.

He started to go to synagogue again, something he had not done since his youth. His folks had been orthodox Jews. Pa had never gone to work on a Saturday. Neither of his parents had ever lifted a finger on the Sabbath, not so much as switched on a light. In the small village in Russia where both his parents had grown up, his paternal grandfather had been a religious Jew of the highest order – a Chassid. As a child, Oscar listened to stories of Chassidic life, Pa's descriptions of Chassidic revelry where the men danced together in a circle, and dipped like candles, and kicked their heels to the tunes of the *Klezmer* – the famous street musicians.

When Oscar married Sandra, he broke with tradition. Money got him hooked to a new lifestyle. On Saturdays, he played tennis in the health club; in winters, he skied on week-ends. He had no time for synagogue on the Sabbath.

Only after Selena left him did he return to synagogue. A reform synagogue this time, where the chanting was less vigorous, and the ladies participated equally with the men. The ceremony was not the same as that in the orthodox *shul* of his youth, but the rituals calmed him and soothed his loneliness.

In synagogue, he prayed for a long life and a large family, though he doubted that his younger daughter Emily, who had declared herself a lesbian, would ever change her orientation and give him grandchildren. At the very least, he wanted to be a part of his existing heritage – his two grandchildren.

Jen clearly had her doubts about letting them stay over in his apartment, as though an aged bachelor's place was hardly a wholesome setting for children. Worse than that, as though he had gotten dimwitted and careless from being alone and might forget the children's basic needs.

A real mother-hen, his older daughter had turned out to be. Too forcefully concentrated on the business of mothering, he often thought, as though something else was missing in her life. She fretted too much about Shawn, about putting enough cookies in his lunchbox, about the Saturday morning cartoons being too violent for him, about the other boys in class scaring him when they roughhoused. She did not permit Shawn to play hockey or baseball, afraid that he would get hurt in spite of the face and head guards.

Oscar thought she overdid it. He noticed that Shawn cried too easily. He did not have enough toughness for a little boy.

In spite of his triumph, Oscar worried about Shawn's reaction to the trip. If Samantha started crying at the cottage, Shawn would join her. Shawn was seven, but he followed his little sister around as though she was the older one.

If Jen would let Oscar have the kids more often, he thought, he would be able to influence Shawn to be more of a leader, more of an athlete too.

When Oscar had married Selena, he wanted to try for a child, but Selena had refused. He did not pressure her; they both had kids from their first marriages, but he still dreamed about having at least one son.

His two daughters had never let him get close enough, he thought, or maybe it was his fault; maybe he had not worked at getting close the way he should have. Jen had been a couch potato as far back as he could remember; he could never get her to ski with him on week-ends, or even to go out skating, no matter what he tried. His Emily had grown-up with her nose in a book; as she grew older, she seemed to become convinced that Dad was an intellectual slouch.

He might never have left the house if there had been a boy at home to keep him company, he thought sometimes, and each time he immediately felt guilty for thinking it. The girls had been a blessing, after all; there was no excuse for his having walked out those many years ago. It was wrong, he knew that. Still, in his first marriage, he had sometimes felt surrounded by girls, clumsy and insufficient somehow, coming home to three women of various ages, waiting for him to satisfy them and finding him wanting every time.

The day seemed to be getting hotter. He could feel pockets of sweat breaking out on his forehead. His head was giving him trouble – sharp needle pricks over the back of his skull.

When he turned up Jen's street, he saw Samantha and Shawn waiting for him on the front lawn, each with a neon-coloured knapsack, and the sharp needles in his skull faded.

It lifted him to see Shawn with his hair slicked over on one side, his freckled face shiny, Samantha near him, posing in a white layered sun-dress with butterfly sleeves. Such handsome children, he thought, and they were his. His own blood. Himself repeated, improved. They would turn out to be smarter than he was, more adaptable, more confident, all-round better. His champions. His blood.

It came to him that grandparenting was the greatest pleasure of all. By the time your children had brought their children into the world, you had made all your mistakes. You were ready for this generation, you could give with your whole heart. He was blessed, he thought; the past did not matter.

He rushed onto the lawn and scooped up Shawn in one arm and Samantha in the other, whirled around with them that way, ignoring the heat, hearing them squeal with excitement.

"Gramps!" Samantha shouted, "I got my three dolls and jammies, and I packed everything all myself."

"Me too," Shawn echoed. "I don't got dolls, but I got toys!"

"Don't have dolls," Oscar corrected.

"Are we going to the water, Gramps?" Samantha's voice was high with joy.

"I can swim." Shawn tugged at Oscar's hand.

"I swim better," Samantha sang.

"We'll see," Oscar said, "when we go to the lake tomorrow."

"Tonight, can we have marshmallows, Gramps?" Samantha asked.

The feeling of pleasure made Oscar breathe heavily; he could feel his eyes tearing.

Jen came out of the house with a box of cookies for them to take along. "Don't let Shawnie swim without his earplugs, Dad," she said. "He gets infections at the drop of a hat."

She had her hand on the top of Shawn's head, as though she took comfort in identifying him as hers. Samantha yanked at her skirt to share in the attention.

The traffic was thick. Everyone in the city seemed to be trying to make a getaway to the cool Laurentian mountains.

People honked all around him, drivers cut him off. Some yelled obscenities at him, but he did not care.

He was taking his time today, driving deliberately slowly; he had precious cargo. The sign posted in his back window said: *Children on Board.* When he was alone, the sign made him feel fraudulent, but today it was genuine.

The whoosh of passing traffic lulled him as he drove.

Renting the modest cottage in the Laurentians had certainly been worth it. He had rented it for them. Now Jen would get used to him taking the kids for week-ends, and she would let it happen more often. He would have as much time with his grandchildren as Sandra did, more maybe.

He invited the kids to sing "Old Macdonald." Samantha shrieked the chorus; Shawn tried to shriek louder.

He could see parts of their heads surfacing in the rear-view mirror as they bounced. Samantha's blue eyes and long lashes; a section of Shawn's forehead; Shawn's small white teeth. He saw for the first time how much Shawn resembled him. The longish Semitic nose, the eyes turned down at the corners, the boy's ears too big like his own. His joy. His *Kaddish* – the one male in the family who would recite the prayers of mourning for his grandfather when the time would come.

Only once did he have to tell them to behave, when he had to get off at a tricky exit, and they were fighting. He raised his voice a little. He noticed Samantha in the mirror biting her lip, and Shawn stiffening and going pale.

After a minute, he invited them to count the trees. They chanted numbers wildly, both of them with shrill voices. Suddenly, something opened up in his mind. The trees became men. He could see them swaying through the corners of his eyes, wise men swaying to music. He heard the chanting of Chassidim, and saw them bending at the waist and praying, bowing their heads in rhythm, praising God. The men were dancing wildly, a *freilich* dance to the festive sounds of the street musicians. The men had formed a circle around him. Oscar saw himself alone in the centre, an old Chassid with a long white beard and traditional prayer shawl wrapped around his shoulders. Thirty-six of his grandchildren were spinning around him, children of all sizes going faster and faster around him, a wheel of fulfilment.

"We're going fast!" Samantha's eager voice sounded a little scared in his ears.

Shawn was imitating the sound of a roaring motor.

"R-r-r! R-r-r! We're speeding!"

Oscar heard glass breaking. A light flashed before his eyes. The light was far too harsh. He tried to cover his eyes, but it did no good. The light was painful, and the dancing around him was making him very dizzy.

Something terrible was happening to him; he knew that. He was sliding to the ground, falling with his heels still kicking out before him. Falling under all the dancing feet.

He heard Samantha shrieking for Mommy. Then she was in his lap, clawing at him, frantic. Both children had been thrown into the front seat. Shawn was there too, bent over at the waist, his head almost touching his bare knees. Oscar could see the neat part in Shawn's hair, the line of scalp, and the little knob at the back of his neck.

The music had died, but Oscar's head kept spinning. He blinked, and tried to concentrate. There were black dots swarming before his eyes, like angry bees unleashed.

He knew. Something had gone berserk in his body, and he had lost hold. He had run them off the road and into this ditch.

He held Samantha close to him, though he could hardly keep his eyes open. He held her close and rubbed her back in circles, and gradually he heard her screams muffling into choking sounds at the back of her throat.

Shawn was absolutely silent. Oscar's throat tightened. Shawn is a big boy, he told himself. He is a big, brave boy. He is holding himself quiet to show his little sister the way to be, to calm her until Gramps finds the way out.

Oscar was drifting again, far away. He tried to talk to the children, not to let himself be carried off, but his words were slurred.

Around them was the raw jutting earth and thick brush. Nothing else. Only the wheels of cars slapping in steady rhythm overhead. They were stuck in this hole underground. As though they were buried alive, and the world was going on above them.

His strength was leaving him, evaporating like air from every pore. He thought about prayer, and the Kaddish prayer came to him.

Yitkadal,
Yitkadash,
Shney,
Rabey . . .

His heart pummelled against his chest. Samantha was pulling hungrily at the cloth of his shirt; she made a suckling noise against him. Her body felt warm and moist, like that of a newborn child.

He blinked his eyes, and looked at Shawn again. He pulled his breath up from his chest. Slowly, he dragged his arm out from beneath Samantha's weight to reach out and touch his grandson.

The boy was cold and still. Oscar kept his hand on his grandson's head. He begged God to let the child live, but, even as he pleaded, he knew that Shawn was dead.

He was dreaming about holding the boy in one arm and whirling him around on his front lawn. I will teach him to pitch, he murmured inside his head, but a wave of sorrow overtook him. I will teach him to catch, he murmured.

Yitkadal,
Yitkadash.

The Kaddish refrain took over.

He altered his prayer. He begged God to take his life too. He prayed as he had never prayed before for God to take him – now, quickly, before any of the living came to save him.

"God – *Adonai* – let me die with him. Let me die with my grandson before they come."

But God would not hear. They were around him, the men with shocked white faces and knowledgeable eyes. They had taken Samantha crying from his arms and wrapped her carefully, and carried her off. They had covered Shawn's face and looked away from the elderly man.

Now, they were prying Oscar out of his car. They were pulling him from behind the wheel where he was stuck. With a special instrument, like a giant-sized crowbar, they were lifting him strapped onto a stretcher, his neck bound tight with heavy wrappings like a shroud. They were taking him this way from his trapped position in the car. To save him, to set him down somewhere else, to serve him up to his suffering.

VERTIGO

The ache creeps at first – little mice paws all over my head. Then it squeezes the sides of my ears and tightens like a rope over the scruff of my neck. It holds me in its grip, and my head spins relentlessly.

"Migraine?" Gary asks.

"And the vertigo too," I say.

"What – again? Why?"

"Dr. Soner tells me that the discomfort often comes out after the acute stress period is over," I say.

My husband does not seem to have heard. "But we just went on vacation," he says.

"Well exactly," I begin – and I don't finish.

"Going to your father's?" He is at the sink now, running cold water over a bowl of strawberries, his back to me.

"Yes – for a few hours."

"And the kids?" He picks up a wet strawberry, inspects it, takes another to check.

"I left them tuna sandwiches and salad for lunch. And those chocolate cream cookies I bought."

"You buy too much junk food," he says. "That white sugar's awful."

"Why don't you feed them then?"

Gary points to his study.

"Believe it or not, I'm looking for a job in there."

"You never find one, though."

"It's only been a few months."

"A year and a half, to be exact."

"I had a good job before."

"Yeah. And how long did you keep that?"

"You're in a mood," Gary says. "Watch how you drive with that head, eh? That car cost a bundle."

"I paid for it." I say.

Gary shakes his head.

In my dead father's house there is dust everywhere. Now that we have lifted the antique china cabinet in his living room and sent it off to be refinished, we see the balls of lint and the mould. Underneath the old double bed with the ornate headboard – the one he stopped sharing with her when I was twelve – we found an intricately woven cobweb. Where the bed stood, there is an exposed patch of raw dull hardwood which had not been scraped and varnished to match the rest of the floor.

"How come this part wasn't finished?" my sister Lorraine asks.

"I don't know. I guess they didn't think anybody would ever look underneath."

We giggle a bit hysterically, Lorraine and I. I remember that my mother giggled inappropriately whenever she was nervous. When our father was angry, on the verge of exploding, she would break down into muffled titters, biting her lips, stopping for a minute and then starting again, close to tears herself.

The bareness here threatens me. I would prefer to let everything stay exactly as it was, to let the dust rest underneath in whatever shape it's assumed. It is dangerous, I think, to uncover these long-hidden corners and to look. But we must, of course. We must take things apart here and be done.

There is nowhere to sit anymore, and so my two sisters and I stand and sip at cokes in cans. I bite into the hard white chocolate which I have brought for the three of us, and see the white crumbs on the floor, and I do not care. This is not his house anymore, though my husband still calls it "your father's."

Since he died four weeks ago, I have been eating compulsively. I have not eaten in this helpless way since my adolescence. My slacks are tight around the bottom; they tug uncomfortably at my stomach. In the last week, two men whistled at me from cars as they drove past, and then I knew I was gaining weight. Strange men leer and whistle only when I'm fat; something about my large undisciplined hips seems to arouse their interest. When I am fashionably slim and in control, they don't even glance.

I told my sisters this when I came in here today, and Anna groaned and warned I'd be sorry if I kept putting it on. "You're trying to hurt yourself, and it's not only since he died. As soon as he stopped eating, you started. I saw."

Lorraine said, "Be grateful for those whistles, Simmie. At our age, there's no sex appeal left."

"Speak for yourself," Anna called out from the far corner of the room. "Simmie's only forty-one. Why shouldn't she look sexy?"

When he took to his bed and stopped talking and swallowing, the two of them argued on the phone a good deal, and wept, and called people for advice. I remained silent; the tears would not come.

I sat beside his bed all week and watched him, I and the nurse we hired. Gary complained about being left alone, but I paid no attention.

Anna went to work each morning; it calmed her nerves, she said. Lorraine called every day and came into the city on the second to last day when we were sure he wouldn't recover. Every half hour I fed him the chalky white protein milk shake for convalescents and watched the liquid linger on his unmoving lips.

Afterwards, the nurse got an eye-dropper – just like you feed baby chicks, she said – and tried to get one drop of moisture into his mouth at a time. It wet his lips, that was all, and he did not seem to know or care.

On the last day, he blinked rapid scissor-blinks all day, let his eyes roll back and up towards the ceiling and made gurgling hard noises in his throat and chest. He seemed to be drifting away – far away from the laboured breathing – and so we gave into it. We took turns sitting beside him and rubbing his long cold hands over and over again. He let his hands fall limp in ours.

While I held his hands, I remembered things which I thought I had succeeded in pushing under. They rose in waves and settled in my throat and made me gag. I swallowed bits of food all day to get the heavy feeling out of my throat, but it did not go away.

"Loser!" she called him once, "Nobody!" she shouted. "I married a nobody!"

His body shook each time he raged. "If I drink, I have every reason! You treat me like dirt. You've always been sorry you married me."

"I smell it all over you! she said. "Ugh! Filthy smell of a drunk!

At the end, all three of us were around him. Lorraine screamed "Dad" and held onto his knees as though she could pull him back, and then she went white and silent. Anna held his hand and felt him tug her towards him as his head slumped over. I stood behind, and held onto her shoulders.

We are dying together, I thought to myself, a chain of

deaths, but my eyes remained dry. Except for the icy cold which wrapped itself around me, my body registered no grief.

Anna sniffs at pieces of my father's clothes. She puts her nose into his herringbone hat, buries her face in his red and white checkered shirt. "Smell," she says. "It's him."

I am repulsed by the gesture but I do not want to hurt her feelings. She cries easily since his death – and so I sniff. It smells of a man's sweat and of detergent, as though one scent could not entirely cancel out the other. And of tobacco – though my father has not smoked for at least fifteen years.

It is the smell I remember when I think of him painting the house during summer vacations, rushing out to the market to bring apricots and walnuts and sweet pink watermelon for us, golden-ribboned boxes of chocolate for her. It is the smell which seemed to cling to the walls and drapes in later years when they fought constantly, and when she finally left him.

"We'll never get rid of it," Anna says, crinkling her nose.

"Why don't we clean the stuff," I say, "and then give it away?"

"Oh no," Anna says fiercely. "I'm keeping his clothes."

"You are?" Lorraine asks. She stands by the window, her hands on her hips now, holding herself apart.

"We'll each of us take a little," Anna says. She scrutinizes Lorraine's face. Then, when Lorraine says nothing, Anna speaks again in a deliberately casual voice. "I could wear this," she holds up a hooded corduroy jacket of his. "Everything's unisex now, anyway."

"I suppose you could," Lorraine says doubtfully.

"How come?" Anna's voice rises aggressively. "You wouldn't wear it yourself, would you?"

"I didn't say I would."

"Then why do you expect me to wear it?"

"I don't expect you to." The corners of Lorraine's mouth tremble. "I just said you could if you wanted to."

Anna decides to abandon the subject. She picks up more of our father's clothes, and folds them away neatly.

When she speaks again, there is daring in her tone, the kind of taunt you hear when children are leading up to a fight.

"How come you don't take something of his, Lorraine? Don't you care about his things?"

"How can I?" Lorraine's voice is almost a whine. "They weigh your luggage on the plane."

"That's not it," Anna snaps.

"What exactly do you mean?" Lorraine's neck is flushed.

"You think you're too good to take something of his, don't you? You think you're so far away from all this." Anna waves wildly to indicate the empty living-room. "So damned superior!"

"Would you leave me alone?" Lorraine screeches so high it hurts my ears. "I don't know what you want from me!"

Anna is the one who starts crying, as though she has lost control of her voice and let out that awful shriek.

Afterwards, when we've taken a walk around the block and felt the breeze building up outside, we come back to it and talk while we work.

"At least, he was peaceful in his old age," Lorraine says.

"Yeah," Anna's face softens. "I gave up so much so he could have a decent life in the end."

"It wasn't that decent," I say suddenly. "He spent the last five years just sitting around."

"That was 'cause he was sick and old. I mean, really, I gave him everything he wanted."

"I know that, Anna. But he didn't have such a great life, that's all I'm saying. Plenty of men his age are still getting around, seeing people, doing things."

"He didn't want to see people . . ."

"He still missed out on a hell of a lot."

"I don't think so," Anna says. "He never complained. It's really a question of what you're used to, isn't it?"

"You mean he got used to being trapped." I am surprised at the bitterness in my voice.

We are all standing quite still now, frightened and expectant, as though we've started something from which we cannot withdraw.

"Remember the time he threatened to kill himself?" I ask.

"Oh no, Simmie, don't." Lorraine's eyes are huge.

"If he had killed himself," I say, "my whole life would have been different."

"For Christ's sake, what the hell are you saying now?"

"If he had gone ahead with it, I wouldn't have married Gary. That's what I'm saying."

"This is crazy," Lorraine says. "We have to stop this. Please."

"It's just strange how things happen," I insist. "That's all. You remember – Gary and I were going to his parent's house that night to announce our engagement. And when that awful business of killing himself started, we cancelled."

"I'm not listening to any more of this shit!" Anna holds her hands over her ears.

"Gary called the engagement off because he was sick and tired of my excuses, he said."

I cannot stop myself from remembering.

"It was when Dad finally came out of the garage that

Mother called Gary to apologize. That night, we moved the wedding date closer."

"Three weeks later, wasn't it?" Lorraine squints.

"Yeah . . . and I never got out again." My voice is weak with anger.

"Oh hell," Anna groans. "Spare me the old regrets."

"You wouldn't have had your kids if you hadn't married Gary," Lorraine says hastily. "Think of that."

"I would have had other kids, with someone else. Someone who can hold down a job," I sneer.

"Don't be so bloody sure of that," Anna's voice rises. "Look at me."

"You stayed with Dad 'cause you chose to, Anna. You made that choice!"

"And what about you?" she shouts. "All that bull you're talking. You married Gary 'cause you wanted to, damn it. You wanted out of here any goddamned way you could, and he was your ticket out!"

"That was a long time ago." I feel my throat tightening, and I know I'm about to cry.

Anna tries to stop the tears. She picks up one of his wool jackets, the pointed-lapel kind that teen-aged boys are wearing these days, and throws it at me. "Take this, Simmie. It would be nice if one of the boys wore something of his. With zoot-suit pants yet," she adds in an effort at lightness.

Lorraine bends over a paper carton. "Let's just close this one up for today and get out of here."

When I get into the house I see Gary in front of the television set watching one of the afternoon talk shows. He turns the set off quickly and calls out to ask me if I checked the tires. And when I tell him I didn't, I didn't have goddamned tires on my mind, he comes out to look at me, takes off his glasses.

"How was it?" he asks.

"Alright, I suppose. Well, awful, of course . . . It's all pretty awful.

"I'm sorry," he says in a solemn voice. He kisses my forehead dutifully. "You smell kind of funny." He moves his head back slightly.

"How?"

"Mothballs, I think. Or tobacco or something. I don't know."

"I smell old, you mean."

"No," Gary says. "You smell like your father." He pauses. "Musty, I suppose."

"Musty?"

"Well, you know what your father's house smelled like. Closed-in. That's it. That's exactly it."

Gary's face brightens with the satisfaction of recognition. He begins to massage my neck with light hands, tries to work the pressure points which my doctor has pointed out to him in the headache chart. "Anyway, you're out of there now, Simmie. You must be relieved it's over, I know."

"It's not over. Not at all."

"What does that mean?"

"I'm still stuck," I say.

Gary looks confused and frightened. When I look into his eyes, the terrifying new dizziness begins. This time, the whole room starts circling around the two of us, getting closer and smaller. For a moment, I lose all sense of where I am – until Gary's spinning head reminds me.

SUGAR

Their names make you think of a sweet thing, cool and sugary on your tongue, like frosted icing or maple syrup. But then something else comes in – a worm working its way through the layer of sweet, or a swarm of ants.

They were twin brothers, almost identical, both a deep chocolate brown colour, with eyes the shade of drifting smoke, and voices smooth as churned butter. Their smell was a mixture of coconut oil and vanilla. Their names were Tambourine and Drummer – Tam and Drums, for short. Those were the names they went by, the only names you knew.

It would make your heart beat too fast each time you had to pass the two brothers on the way to the corner. Each time you passed, they said something special to you, the words rolling off their tongues or coming from deep inside their throats. Sweet nothings, people might call them, but they were something to you, you had never heard such pretty things said.

"Sugar," they said. "Sweet pea."

"Honey plum."

"Little buttercup," they called out.

They laughed deep, deep in their throats, moist warm laughter, not derisive like other men's laughter. The brothers were neighbourly; neighbourliness was a part of their greeting. On the block, they were known as all-around good sports, the kind who would help an older person across the street or take a housewife's heavy bags and carry them all the way to her front stoop.

You heard that they were twenty-two years old, but it was hard for you to tell their ages.

You had just turned thirteen. When Ma had you, she was forty-one; you were her miracle child. God had not closed the door on her, she often said, God had kept the door open for her just a little longer. Each time she said this, you pictured God with one hip against a closing door, holding it open, last-minute, for Ma.

The brothers were so handsome, with muscles running across their backs and hips, and glistening dark eyes – it was hard to think of them as parents like your own, but they were. They had two children between them – a toddler belonging to Drums, and an older boy of about four with milk-coffee skin and thick eyelashes who belonged to Tambourine.

They were married to sisters, pale women with auburn hair and wide green-grey eyes. The women were not twins, but they looked almost the same – thin lips stained burgundy red, and wavy hair that ran halfway down their backs. The wives tried to be neighbourly too, calling out hello to people, but it was not the same. They did not have the style. Their words came out separate, not at all melted together and soothing like their husbands' greetings.

The brothers came from Tennessee and spoke what people on the block called "American." It sounded exotic to you, foreign and titillating.

When they laughed or called out, their bodies danced.

"Hah, hah . . . yeah." The brothers laughing their honeyed laughter out loud, bent over at the waist, stomping their feet with enthusiasm.

It was a pretty thing to see them on the block, the brothers and their wives and the two boys they had between them. A twin family, you thought, living all together in a small base-ment flat. Everyone on the street was poor, and they were too, but they did not show it. They looked to you – leaning against the fender of their old red Chevy convertible, lowering their heads to talk, flashing wide smiles – like entertainers. Like they had been invited to a long party on the block, and the party would go on as long as they stayed.

It is a difficult time, the summer you turn thirteen, your period come on like a disease, blood trickling down your leg and clotting on your underwear, making you feel soiled.

When you were younger, Pa used to rub his fingers slowly over your head and the back of your neck, like he was spelling you a secret. Saying you were his precious little Jeannie, perfect Jeannie, you were still the one.

Now, he does not touch you anymore. You catch him looking at you at the breakfast table when you are wearing the tight ribbed tank top which Ma bought you at *Kresge's*. He looks at you like he has seen something not-nice, a salt-stain under a sweaty armpit. He turns away fast, spreads his fin-gers tight around his coffee cup, absorbing the heat.

You used to sit on his lap, but that is not allowed any-more. Nothing is said, it is understood.

Even Ma lowers her eyes these days when you come out to the kitchen wearing your frilly baby-doll pyjamas, thin straps on the shoulders slipping off. You wet your lips; you know how good you look. You have looked at yourself hard in your bedroom mirror, marvelled at the long legs, the little bones jutting out just perfect on your shoulders, the naked smoothness of your upper arm. You forget the blood-stains on your underwear; none of it is so ugly when you see yourself mirrored this way.

You want Pa to look up from his paper and tell you how

pretty you are. How grown up. His precious. Papa's girl. But he does not say anything.

Ma says, "Jeannie, please. We're having breakfast dear, go get dressed" – her face screwed tight like her bunions are pinching.

At night, in front of the mirror, you put on lipstick, and you line your eyes with Ma's *Kohl* pencil. You try on all your baby dolls, your nightie with the spaghetti straps, your two tiny new brassieres with matching panties. You make faces as you have seen fashion models do in magazines; you pout into the mirror, you open your eyes wide. You jut one hip out to the side. You lean forward from the waist, making your small breasts swell.

You lay out your clothes each night for the brothers, so you will look delicious when you go out on the street next day. You choose and match – soft pink halter to go with hot pink shorts. Daffodil blouse with yellow pedal pushers that lie especially snug around the waist and hips.

You walk past them next day, rotating your hips, like that is the way you get from one place to the other, that is just the way you walk. You remember to keep wiggling long after you pass them. You know they are watching, you can feel their eyes following you.

They make wet noises in their throats.

"Fine fox," Tambourine says.

His brother clicks his tongue. "Hah – hah – yeah!"

"Buttercup all grown up, these days," Tambourine says. "Switching those hips like waves."

"I'm bored," you say to him one day, a little make-believe whine in your voice, trying to sound like a spoiled rich girl. It has just come to you to say what you do, you have not planned this part.

"You what?"

"B-O-R-E-D!" You spell the letters out for him, brazen.

"Why's that, honey?"

"My daddy won't let me go out on a single date," you say. "Not even one. I'm old enough, but he doesn't understand." None of this is true; you have not been asked out on a single date, and you do not even call Pa "Daddy," you never have. You sound like someone else, another person you have just made up.

"My," Tambourine says soberly. "My-my."

"Well, what do you think?" you ask him. "Don't *you* think I'm old enough?"

Tambourine laughs, a thin scared sound. "School start pretty soon, don't it?" he asks his brother.

Drums, looking back at him, says, "Young lady can hold on till then, I'm certain."

They don't call you "baby" next day, or "buttercup," or "sugarplum." None of that.

"Morning, Jeannie," is all they say, and they look down at their shoes.

You are sitting in an abandoned shed in the back yard next to your house, old rags stacked up to make a kind of seat, and Tambourine's jacket folded behind your head to make you a cushion. The house connected to the shed is empty; the big Italian family that lived there moved away. From where you are sitting, you can see the crooked back porch and the large green bottles which the Italian lady left behind. She used to make home-made wine in these bottles. You went to visit one time with Ma, and the wine was served. It seems so long ago. You sat with Ma on that porch, and the Italian lady gave you sweet flaky pastry with nuts in it and powder on top. You were just a little girl, braids woven tight and gathered on the top of your head. Pinafore dress. Leaning against Ma's leg. Protected. You almost wish you could be that little girl again.

You lean against Tambourine, your head snuggled into the hollow of his arm. He rubs your back in small circles. You feel like a small kitten in his hands. You want to make purring sounds inside your throat.

"Baby-cat," he whispers, just like he has heard you thinking. You are too shy to look into his face.

Nothing that is happening to you now is real. You can see Tambourine's shiny knuckles and the pinkish palms of his hands in the dark. While he strokes you, you can hear Ma and Pa talking softly to each other in the quiet dusk, as though they are right beside you. They are right there, sitting together on their back balcony. If you peeked, you would see them.

Even while Tambourine whispers "Baby, pretty baby, soft sweet baby" in your ear, you can hear Ma telling Pa she needs new linoleum for the kitchen floor.

"You see in the corner there?" she says. "You see the red squares all worn out? It's time to buy new, Dave! We can't wait."

Pa says he will see, for the holidays maybe. When he pauses in his talk, you can picture exactly what he is doing – what he does every time Ma asks for something that costs money. He rubs the knuckles of one hand with the other. He has arthritis in his fingers, that is why he can no longer work two shifts at the machine shop.

Worry makes the arthritis hurt more, he says; but Ma says talk of money makes him ache. She says that only when they are having an argument – not now. Now they are sitting calmly on the back balcony, Ma in her white apron, Pa wearing his brown orthopaedic slippers, one leg crossed over the other. Thinking Jeannie is at her friend Helen's house playing Monopoly, while they drink orange soda, and look out at the bit of sky darkening over the back sheds.

It makes your heart leap to picture them so close to where you are. If you wanted to run out of the shed right now, you could not do it. They would see your shadow spilling across the yard. If the shed started to burn now, if it lit up in flame against the sky, you would just have to squat in the heat and be scorched to death; you could not run.

The goose bumps come out like little cat paws all over your arms and legs and down your back. You feel like peeing, like the time you were on the roller-coaster ride in the park. You cross your legs tight together to forget.

Tambourine puts one hand between your legs and pushes them apart. He does this easily, as though he could do it with one hand behind his back. It makes you want to cry, his fingers moving light up and down your inner thighs, ticklish feather-touch that makes you want to scream out loud.

He kisses you full and hard on the mouth, as though to keep your voice from running away. Like the plug that goes into the bathtub to stop the water from running out – that is how Tambourine stuffs your mouth with his tongue.

Pa is saying he will have a glass of boiled milk with froth before bed tonight; he was tired at the shop today. You hear Ma sigh for an answer. Tambourine is whipping his tongue, pointy and small like a spear, fast in and out of your mouth and your ear, so fast you do not know anymore what is going where.

You feel the throbbing between your legs and again on the pulse inside your wrists.

Your head is pounding like it will burst open and spill.

His nostrils are wide, his eyes watery in the dark. He smooths over the lines of your cheeks, he touches your eyes with his fingertips, and whispers.

"Jeannie. Jeannie baby. I been wanting you bad." His breath catches in his throat.

He presses his fingers hard against you again, in the place where he is not supposed to be. You are afraid he will hurt you. He will break something inside, something will break, and then what will you do.

It is your voice that breaks instead, you feel yourself shudder, and hear yourself quiver-cry. A wild cry, like a burnt thing. A small thing bruised.

Ma and Pa have gone. You no longer hear their voices; they have taken their chairs inside for the night.

He bites your mouth. "Baby, ba-by," he moans like he is drowning. "Run on home now!" He shoves you a little, hoarse, frantic, afraid of something. "Go on!" he says. "You first. Don't tell, you hear?"

You duck and run that way out of the shed and straight across the back yard, bent over at the waist. Up to the front of the street, up the stairs to the house, with your face closed tight, and your breath coming hard.

It is four days since you have been out of the house. You do not dare go into the street. Your face will turn beet red if you meet him, your voice will come out wobbly, you will make a fool of yourself and spoil everything.

It is better to pretend you have a fever, and to stay inside near the window watching him from upstairs. Remembering.

You go over everything in your head. You taste each moment over again, suck at it like hard candy on your tongue, the flavour of it rushing like heat to your ears.

You have a heartbeat between your legs. A regular steady heartbeat. Right there, where he touched. Four days, and the heartbeat is still going.

All day long, you peek from your window and see him there – smoking a cigarette, narrowing his eyes against the smoke, squinting. Squinting. Thoughtful. Waiting for you.

The fourth night, the noise starts. You hear him from inside his basement flat, shouting in a mean, foreign voice.

"You got that?" he shouts. A menacing sound. Taunting. Like stomping on your foot to scare a small animal. "You ain't going to get away this time, boy!"

"I didn't." You hear his son saying that one thing over and over again weakly, his voice shaking. "I didn't, Daddy. I didn't."

Scuffling noises, the boy crying. Him bullying, mocking the boy. "Get over here, you! Chickenshit, ain't you?"

You hear the hard blows raining down on the boy, the sound of leather on bare skin, the father's bitter voice, caustic, someone else. "I told you, didn't I?" The boy choking back sobs, and crying, begging. "Please, Daddy. Please, please, Daddy, no."

You cover your ears. You know it is your fault. He is beating the boy because of you. There is some terrible connection; you do not know what it is, but you know it is so.

Slut. Dirt-maker. Trouble-maker. You know these words, you have heard them used in school about the older girls, the ones who do dirty things with boys.

You remember a fight Pa had with Ma once. "Lousy dames start the trouble," he said. "Each and every time! They get a man started, and then the poor jerk is left holding the bag!" He did not think you heard.

Your bachelor uncle Walt. Drinking whisky in the kitchen with Pa until late at night, talking man-talk by the table long after you and Ma had gone to bed.

"Every one of them the same," Uncle Walt said. "In the daytime they're one thing. Nights, it's something else. They'll do anything. Once they get hot between the legs, they don't care about nobody!"

Everything is ugly now. The time in the shed, the kisses, the heartbeat between your legs, the crying pleading boy. All of it ugly. The lovemaking and the beating. You cannot think of one without the other.

When Ma heard the noise in the street, she came to your bedroom window and stood beside you and listened. She pulled at the ends of her hair and said, "God . . . for God's sake . . . he is going to kill that boy." Her voice started to rise.

She put her arms around you, saying, "We must do something," not knowing what to do. She held you tight to her, and said, "Jeannie, oh Jeannie, baby, You're shaking. Jeannie, please. You're making me cry too."

You never told Pa about the tumult, he slept right through.

Now, years later, you and Ma often talk together about things that happened on the block.

You remember the neighbours. The Italian lady who served wine, the Ukrainian man who made borscht and invited the whole family, the dog that froze in the back lane. You remember Pa's getting sick right after you moved away, like moving away was a bad-luck thing to do.

You and Ma talk about the kids on the block, how one grew up to become a policeman, and one a gangster, and one of them – the toughest and wildest of them all – was now running for mayor, for goodness' sake.

You refuse to talk about the night you heard the beating, you and Ma, the night both of you huddled and cried together with your elbows on the windowsill, looking out into the street for a long long time after it had all died down. Neither of you mentions that night.

You both know it is something to be buried and shovelled under. It would carry too much shame to unearth it and drag it up to the surface again.

RICE CASTLE

I remember Michael when his eyes shone green; they used to sparkle when I talked. He'd smile and watch me when I ate.

He loved my eyebrows – an uplifting arch, he said. "Are they your own?" he'd tease. "You sure? They're the most expressive eyebrows I've ever seen, Melissa. Honest."

Michael loved my stories, the little anecdotes I used to tell. He never tired of them. His favourite story was the story of the bell-fringed tambourine, the one I stole out of my kindergarten class when the teacher wasn't looking. I took it home tucked into my snowsuit, muffling the sound of the bells with my mittened hands clutched tight against my chest.

"Odd wasn't it, Michael, to steal it?" I asked. "Really strange for a five-year-old to do that, no?"

"A little dreamer," Michael said. "It's perfect. I love it." He laughed. "Reach for those tambourines, Melissa. Don't ever stop. Beautiful."

Everything I did pleased him. My impulsiveness expressed a special part of my personality, he always said. My unorthodox behaviour revealed my energy, my natural excitement about life – he explained to me. I could do no wrong.

Now he criticizes me a lot. His eyes are flat. He grunts to himself at the breakfast table, and eats with his face close to the plate. He drinks frequently, but he never gets happy. He snaps at me because I use toilet paper to wipe my nose. "Can't you afford some Kleenex, Melissa?"

He gets upset about the way I slice the cheese, sneers

when my coffee's not strong enough. "This is like hot tap water. It doesn't do a thing for me," he says. He clears his throat frequently when I'm around, a dry muffled sound, as though something chokes him. He shuts me out of his study, closes the door quietly and paces in there like a caged animal.

Sometimes he sits in the dark living room for hours and smokes after I've gone to bed. His tension makes my body stiff. His smoke rings sting my eyes.

I don't know when it happened. Maybe a month ago, after his thirty-eighth birthday. When I mention the change and suggest seeing a doctor, he dismisses me angrily.

"Stop taking my emotional temperature, for Christ's sake! Haven't you ever been down?" he shouts. "I'm not top-of-the-world these days. So what? I'm human. You want me to be euphoric all the time?"

I console myself by thinking of him as he was before – when he was married to Samantha and we were just good friends.

Sometimes we relax together and talk about the good old days. Do you remember when?

"Remember those sexy high-heeled boots you used to wear when we first met? I used to worry about you on the ice, you know. I never told you, but I always thought you'd fall."

"I used to lean on you though, remember?"

"Right."

"And you loved it, Michael, didn't you?"

"Right."

"I still have those boots," I venture.

"Yeah . . . well," he mutters. "Remember that scarlet pink thing you wore to Jeremy's reception, Melissa? Fantastic!"

I couldn't dare wear it now, Michael, I think to myself.

Now you might squint and say that whore-pink colour hurts your eyes.

"You remember those shirts we shopped for, Michael? Afterwards, I started trying on the men's sailing jackets in red and yellow and green and mauve. I was so happy that day, I roamed around the store like a peacock. The salesman was getting a bit upset, I think."

"No, he wasn't," Michael protests. "He was enjoying you. I was too. That was a treat watching you modelling all those colours. That was special."

I wouldn't do that now, Michael, I think to myself. You'd knock me down in a second. You'd spoil everything with your weary sighs of disgust.

"Remember those lunches, Melissa?"

"God, yes. Those leisurely four-hour lunches. We took so much time together then."

"The best part was watching your eyes." He laughs in the old way. "Do you know that ginger chicken with orange slices would actually make your eyes shine?"

"We could go for ginger chicken together right now, Michael," I urge. "And eat it with our fingers like we used to."

"You were so oral then, Melissa," he says dreamily. "I mean you gave a whole new meaning to food."

I still am, Michael, I think to myself – only now I'm afraid you'll wince when I chew.

"Remember that editor who critized my article so harshly, Michael? You were so supportive, you defended my work so well."

"But your work was great, Melissa, and you had such a lot of courage. You really stood up for your rights that time."

I still would, Michael, I think to myself – only now I'm afraid you'd think I'm aggressive.

"I used to dream about you," Michael says, "all the time."

"I used to imagine seeing you," I say, "in the most un-likely places, at the most impossible times."

"Remember the tea *flambée?*" Our eyes widen simultane-ously, a flare of recognition. The flame is sputtering, we're burning out. My God. We talk about each other as though we're dead now, as though those two people are strangers, two lovers we knew in the past. That's when we stop usually, when we see ourselves mirrored in each other's eyes, startled and sad, and Michael's eyes start narrowing, and my throat starts closing and my head feels tight.

We let it go at that point always – the breaking point. But we come back to it from time to time.

On nights when it rains and we feel washed clean, or Michael's gone swimming and his limbs feel young, we cud-dle up and talk again. Remember the bookstore where we met? Ghost stories.

We don't talk about Samantha, though. Every time I want to, Michael cuts me off. "She's not your problem, Melissa," he says. "I made the choice, remember? And she's fine." But she weighs heavily. I feel her there.

She comes over sometimes. She brings delicate gifts: decorative placemats and candle-holders. She's quiet and gracious. She seems to accept our relationship. Maybe she's hiding her feelings – but I don't think so. That's the way she is, I think; that's the way she always was. She's calmer than I am, more peaceful.

Michael is sweet and gentle when she's visiting. He's tender to both of us. He needs us both, and I like her. Some-times I wish she'd move in here with us. She's part of this arrangement. She's not just a guest. Sometimes I think I should slip our the back door when she's here, tell Michael and her I'm going to get cigarettes, and never come back. Peace. A kind of peace.

We're having some friends over to dinner, some of Michael's academic friends. I cook a meal, and Michael helps me. He's happy while we're busy in the kitchen together. He's boyish and content, proud of me, looking forward to a great evening.

I prepare his favourite foods – mussels in a creamy white wine sauce, loads of garlic, more than enough white wine, red onion. I've made a well in the middle of the rice, poured some of the mussels and cream sauce in the middle, then turned the glass bowl carefully upside down, so the rice looks like a child's handiwork in the sand. As a child, I used to love doing that on the beach: fill up my pail with sand, pack it in firmly, turn it upside down, and see the sculpted sand cake.

I bite the tip off a round raw mushroom, and arrange the remaining mussels and cream sauce around the tall rice castle. Michael kisses my ear lightly as I perch a perfectly scalloped half-lemon on top of the rice. I sprinkle some fresh green mint leaves on the lemon, playfully sprinkle parsley on Michael's hair, and stop to kiss him.

The salad's crisp and colourful: shiny cherry tomatoes, baby onions, avocado slices, mint leaves, perky broccoli heads tucked into lettuce leaves. Michael puts his hand into my hip pocket, pours me some wine, and kisses my forehead.

We're fresh and excited when our friends arrive. Everyone is thirsty, the chilled white wine is perfect. Michael's body is relaxed. He doesn't tense his shoulders, he doesn't tighten his brow, he doesn't choose his words with that rigid defensive caution he gets when he's nervous. The sun shines in brightly through the wide windows. Michael smiles at me from across the room.

I haven't seen him looking so happy and free since our leisurely four-hour lunches. I'm famished.

The dry season's over, I think to myself; it was worth it, all of it. This is how I always wanted it to be for us.

The laughter flows around the table. The talk in the room is spontaneous and easy. Everyone here is catching on to the spirit of celebration. They may not know what it is, but I do. Michael's rejuvenation. The rhythm in the room is more important than the words. Someone says something simple about feeling good, someone else says something about the texture of mussels.

Michael toasts me. "Here's to the best friend I have," he says.

I bring out more mussels in sauce and everyone digs in. The rice castle collapses finally as Michael scoops up a last spoonful from the serving plate. Some of the guests lean back; others light cigarettes and move out to the living room to settle down.

Michael brings out brandy and puts on a Dylan record. Dylan's lyrics – "You gotta serve somebody" – fill the room. A few people listen carefully, and others start to talk amongst themselves.

I am getting sleepy – a warm comfortable feeling. This might be the first night for real sleep in months. Michael starts to talk about Dylan's religious period to the young woman beside him, and then I hear her say something solemn about loyalty. The word wakes me up like a danger signal, and I move in quickly and say something about the fresh breeze coming in through the window.

Michael cuts me off though. He avoids my eyes, tightens his jaw muscles, and starts an earnest discussion about loyalty and self-respect. "You have to make a commitment to one person in your life," he says, "and respect yourself for sticking to it."

Everything turns sour then. Michael stops talking completely; I recognize the panic in his face. He lights a cigarette and squints. He looks around the room while the others talk, searching out the shape of the ceiling, as though he feels sealed in. He swallows hard.

I'd like to make him feel better by asking him to play his guitar, but that is impossible, I can tell.

Food might do it, I think. Something elemental. I remember the fancy dessert I prepared. Glazed peaches in Tia Maria. Sweet food – an omen of good things, I think. I bring it out to the living room and offer it to our guests. My hopes for peace disintegrate when Michael speaks.

"You've bruised the peaches," he says. "You've spoiled the whole dessert."

"What's really wrong, Michael?" I ask. "Please talk to me about it."

"Nothing's wrong," he says in a bitter voice. "You've just bruised the peaches."

There is embarrassed silence in the room.

When the guests have left, I feel sober. "It isn't any good, is it, Michael?" I say to him. "Maybe you should go back to Samantha. Maybe you'd feel better. Nothing's final yet."

"I can't," Michael says. "We're stuck together. Can't you see?"

"You can go back, Michael. Do it. It's better that way. Really. This whole thing's unnatural. You should be with Samantha. That's what's bothering you . . ."

Michael spits his words out. "That's what you said before. Remember? 'This whole thing's unnatural,' you used to say. 'Her or me,' you used to say. 'You can't hang on to both of us,' you always said. I warned you that it wouldn't be easy. But you were so sure of yourself." He chuckles contemptuously. "'Conviction' – that was your favourite word. You had so much 'conviction.'" He looks at me with menacing eyes. "Now you're stuck with me, see? I'm the prize."

Then his tone changes, and he sounds like a broken, fragile boy. "Everything I touch turns to shit," he murmurs. He looks bewildered, reaches out to touch my hand, then pulls his hand away as though he is scared of being burned.

"I'm sorry, Michael. But we can change it. It's probably my fault."

I expect Michael to protest. I expect him to say we both made the choice like two adults, but he doesn't.

"You should have stopped with the kindergarten tambourines," he snaps. "You should have just let it go at that."

He picks up the bowl of abandoned rice and runs his hand calmly and protectively around the circle of its smooth ceramic rim.

SONG FOR A DEAF MAN AND HIS MUTE
DAUGHTER

When you were sick, weak and damp with fever, I heard a love song on the radio and danced around your bed. You squinted up at me with your bloodshot eyes and spoke in a raspy voice: "You're dancing, Sarahle? Your father is getting better, this means." You smiled then for the first time during your illness; after that you started to improve.

When you were alive, I could make connections only if I spoke directly into your ear. If I spoke with conviction in an even clear voice, you allowed me into your life, and we both felt better.

I am not getting better, Pa. Since you have gone, it is impossible for me to fix on things that are being said. I have become mute. There is a constant din in my head and I try not to listen to it. I hear the sounds you must have heard in your darkness, but I am not sure they are the same. I lie in my bed and close everything out.

This song to you may be the answer, the broken splintered song of a mute woman pasting together the pieces of a life and death. If I can gather the separate notes and dance with enough truth and grace around your spirit, they will perhaps come together. If I sing it with enough love, the broken sounds will not matter so much; you will hear and you will let me in.

You will liberate me into my mourning.

I sit beside your bed and watch you blinking, sometimes gazing straight ahead. You do not respond to my gestures, my urging you to eat, to drink a little at least. I hold the glass of vitamin-bolstered vanilla milkshake to your lips. A half of this tiny glass may extend your life by an hour. Useless, this bit of nursing my sister Nissa and I indulge in. You are weak beyond repair; the doctors told us that. These mothering gestures are necessary for us. We cannot abandon our efforts on your behalf, even after we have abandoned hope.

While I monitor your fading life, I grieve my mother's death. She, dissatisfied, died harder than you do. She was a worrier, ambitious and strong. She wanted to leave her house in order. To her, that meant leaving her children provided for. She worried that she was leaving me behind unwed. A thirty-year-old woman, without a man to take care of her, without children to fulfil her. I made her dying more difficult; the pain which ravaged her body could not distract her from motherly anxiety. At the last, I think – I hope – it did distract her. She closed her eyes and relinquished me – spat at the pain. Hissed at it, felt her breath catch in her throat, and expired.

You do not have to dismiss me so forcefully. You are better at dying than Ma was; you are better at acceptance than Ma could ever be.

I give you another sip of milkshake which stains your purplish lips white. The liquid lingers on your mouth, your full mouth, sensuously shaped.

It begins to settle in me then, the hurt you felt when you were denied love. "You don't let me hold up my head," you used to say to her. "I walk around with a bent head." She shamed you into submission, she had no other choice. She broke you and then felt sorry for the wounded broken thing you had become.

You fought badly: you rammed and butted with your head down instead of courting her back to the light – gently, openly. You cursed in your drunkenness, and she hid from you. You went looking for her in dark closets when you came home from the tavern, wanting to tear at her for the things you had lost.

I understand it more than you probably know, Pa. It was hard to be a man then. It was hard to find your manhood. You knew very little praise, except with the men in the tavern. I know what that was like. It was the way of my adolescence, the way I discovered my limited power. In the dark clubs with the music pounding into my heart, I learned of my womanhood and was intoxicated by the night. In the Hot Blues Club I smelled that fragile triumph.

I did not know before then that my body could be considered a jewel. As a child sitting on the front stoop, I knew only that my hands were stained and my nails bitten down, that my chubby bare knees were dimpled and exposed shamefully to the businessmen from the West Side of the city who drove down the block. To them I was a slum child – a slum girl child – and that meant I would be easily impregnated one day, then kept on in the dreary service of a working man, with his head forever bent away from the light.

In the Hot Blues club I was no longer a slum child watching from the shadows. Men praised me with their eyes.

You knew that kind of praise in the tavern. With the rowdy men around you, rough and affectionate, you ordered rounds of beer, foamy-headed beer which caked on your mustache. Later in the night, sandwiches, harsh peppers and pickles, extra-spicy foods which only a strong man could swallow. Toothpicks and cigars afterwards, used jauntily and openly.

In the tavern they called you Davey, some nicknamed you Sport. They joked with you about the women you had on the side, women you dreamed about but never courted. They told lewd stories of their sexual prowess, stories of violence in which men were men and women were always kept underfoot. It was your time, Pa. It was a way out of the dreariness for a few hours every Friday night.

I see you sitting among them, listening to them swear in Ukrainian and French and Polish and English, forgetting that you had not succeeded in this country, that other immigrants who had come here with you had risen fast and strong and left you behind, that now your wife scorned you, that your children sometimes avoided you. In the boisterous tavern, with chairs scraping along the tiled floor, with the smell of beer, with the trays of sparkling glasses delivered to you at the round table, you lost the taste of defeat.

Outside that tavern when you stumbled onto the sidewalk and blinked at the natural light, you were robbed of your courage.

In thirty years you never missed a day of work.

At five every morning when we all lay in bed, you got up, slicked your hair back with a wet comb, washed your face with cold water in the kitchen sink, and scurried away.

You got to the factory before your boss, waited outside the door for him to come and open up. It was the fear of not pleasing the bosses that drove you, the fear of not getting to work on time, not paying your rent in time, the shame of being evicted by landlords.

You were never freed of that burden until you were too old to enjoy your freedom. By the time you could scoff at obligations, your rasping lungs had confined you to the armchair which had become your home. Often, in the last few months, you were startled out of your dozing reverie, jolted out of senility by a sudden memory of past responsibilities.

"I have to go to work?"

We would have to tell you, Nissa and I, that you were retired, you were cared for, you would always be nourished by us. Finally, you would lean back in your chair relieved, your breathing become less shallow. You would accept a cup of coffee rich with melted sugar and cream, and smile at us, a baby's toothless grin.

And then the jagged line of panic would work its way through again, and your hands would begin to tremble. Your long fingers would clasp at your beard, your forehead crease itself into pleats of worry; you would narrow your eyes and bleat: "The rent! Did I pay the rent?"

Your hands felt clammy and awkward. At the dance hall you retreated to your sister's side, kept your distance from all the prettier women, waltzed near the shadows with the older ones, the ones who couldn't cut you down.

Until you met her, my mother. The pretty little one with delicate features and dark sad eyes turned down at the corners. The one feverish with ambition and dazed with anxiety. The talented one of her family who had arrived first from Russia, had been stolen across by a relative, and had slaved to bring her family over one by one. Shayna, the one who was later scorned by her sisters for her beauty and superiority. They huddled together and left her alone. Until the fear of isolation overtook her and she blindly sought a mate.

You couldn't believe your luck; she was too splendid for you, you said. Too polished. It would take effort to keep up with her. She frightened you, you wouldn't risk it.

Then you bent to please her, and let yourself be led.

You surrendered to her and finally you came to believe it had always been this way: you forgot your caution and blundered. When your failures were obvious, your shame made you mean. You compounded mistakes to prove something to her. You made yourself ugly, as ugly as you felt she was unforgiving. Until she despised you and pitied herself.

"Limp," she said. "Nobody! You're a nobody to me. A nothing I married."

She moved into the back room with us, your children.

She laughed whenever you attempted to do something nice for her.

Nissa comforted her, and you turned to me for comfort.

I sponged your forehead with cold compresses after you had thrown up, I covered you with an extra blanket, I snuggled into your bed beside you when you seemed lonely.

When I became a woman and you an elderly man, you reached for me when you were ill. "Hold me, Sarahle." I bolted from the room and hated you, then hated myself for my meanness. Spent days weeping over your frailty, hovered over you, sat by your bedside for hours, spoon-feeding you ice cream, holding your hand.

"You won't leave me?" you asked constantly. "You won't move off to another city? You don't want a man, Sarahle. Do you? You want to be with your father. Don't you? You and your sister, both."

Your death. How can I sing of that? The memory is blurred by pain, it punishes me in the night. I felt nothing at the time, Pa, only a quiet sense of relief.

"I am breathing hard," you whispered. "I am dying." Your eyes were wide and calm. There was no fear in your voice. Just before you died you fathered me by urging me to find my life. You released me.

As you gave yourself over to the force which courted you, you handed me over – graciously, generously – to the destiny which awaited me.

We both knew that your death meant my life. That I had been waiting for many years. Waiting for my freedom.

Then I forgot everything. The gift you gave me turned heavy and dark in my hands after you left.

I did not know what to do with it.

UNDERGROUND

In this long dark tunnel, this endless black hole, I know she is upon me. She follows me everywhere, she slows me down, and holds me. She will not let me go.

"We are sad," she says. "We are all of us sad. We have no luck. Never any luck."

I thought I had left her long ago, but she has caught me again. She caught up with me when I was going through a lost hard time. She dug her fingernails hard into the palms of my hand, and held my wrist with a grip like a handcuff and said, "See? You are down now. You are down. And so you know. You are just like me. A sad woman. With a bad man by her side. A mean man. They are all mean – those we find. Other women get good men, kind men, but not us. No. We get cruel men. Awful cruel men who do not care for us. They care only for others."

When I tell her I am having a hard time just now, but it is temporary, I will get out, she smiles a satisfied grin and says, "You are like me. He treats me like dirt."

"I am not like you," I say. "He does not treat me like dirt. That is not what I am saying."

"You are sad as I am," she says. Her mouth is pinched and hard. Relentless.

"Oh yes," she goes on. "I never was happy. No luck. None. No luck at all. What a beautiful bride I was. If only I had another chance to start over. God, I was gorgeous. Gorgeous," she repeats. "So slim and lovely. Absolutely gorgeous!" She gorges herself on the word.

Her voice is a whisper. The whisper turns into a whistle and then a scream. The scream rises in the air, and snags itself in my hair. It nests in my hair, so we are tied together. Strands of hair tighten us to each other, and I can go nowhere without her.

She follows me everywhere, in the dark, always in the dark. She tries to stay behind so I will not know she is doing it, following me and holding onto me, slowing me down so I cannot get away. Not before her.

"Wait," she says behind me. "Do you know how lonely I was the nights he did not come home. Late, late, the small hours of morning, the sky turning white, and he was still not there."

I pretend not to hear, and keep walking. It is dangerous to hear. If you stop, she will tell you more, and then more, until you are caught in her story, and have nothing of your own left anymore. It will all be her story, so that you have nothing of yourself and you do not count. If you stop and let yourself, she will swallow you.

I keep walking. Sometimes I murmur things. "I am sorry," I say. "It is too bad he did not make you happy."

"What a bastard he is," I say sometimes, just to appease her. "Too bad," I murmur politely. I keep on walking, but it is not enough.

She pulls at my skirt. "But you don't know everything," she says. "There is more. He did not ever speak to me. Not really. In truth, he pretended I was dead. We were like two ghosts in the same house. When he wanted to, at night, he crawled on top of me, and took me. He did not ask. He did not care where I hurt."

I keep walking, I mutter polite agreements, but I am stuck underground with her. I cannot get into the light.

She wants us to be twins. She tries to look like me. She

pins her hair up as I do and twists it in a knot. She applies dusky eye shadow just as I do. She wears my scents. She tries to stay young by losing weight. I see her silhouette along the walls of the underground now. She wears very high-heeled shoes. She has become tiny. She has shrunk so she can appear younger and look like me.

I will not let her mimic me. I do not want her to mirror me and so I toss off my high-heeled shoes and walk barefoot.

I stop suddenly at a pastry shop in the underground and buy six éclairs and twelve mille-feuilles and seven cream puffs at once and gorge myself. Then three marzipans for good measure. Good. I eat them all without even a cappuccino for my thirst. When I look at my own silhouette against the wall of the underground, it is wide. My hips have spread clear across the corridor, my legs are swollen, my cheeks unusually puffy, my eyes small slits. I feel nauseous from all the pastry, and the shape of my body sickens me, but I am glad to be so monstrously fat. At least, I do not look like her. I cannot be said to look like her. She is svelte, and I am not. I am not. She cannot knot me to her.

She follows me past the lit windows with the dummies in them. She stops when I stop. She is making my heart beat far too fast. She is still behind me. Her shadow mocks me. It spreads around my feet like a dirty puddle. Sad dirty puddle.

Suddenly, I whirl around to face her head-on, though whirling is not so easy now that I have gotten so fat.

She does not seem to notice how fat I have become in the last ten minutes. She does not care. I was slim ten minutes ago, a size nine, like her. She worries about her size, prides herself on being a seven sometimes. She gets on the scale every morning, she makes herself throw up if the scale goes up, but she does not worry that I have just become a size 24½. Senior-Senior – huge size. Extra-Over-size. She does not care.

One man passing, yells "Hey there, Fatso. Where'd do you get them buns?" His wife tugs his coat sleeve enthusiastically and jeers. "Hawg!" she calls out. "Big fat hawg."

Another man, thinking I am hurt, stops me and puts his arm around my shoulder. "Listen here, Honey," he says. "I don't mean no offense, but I seen you ten minutes ago, sweetheart, looking like a genuine person! Now I've come down this tunnel, and you've turned into a Queen-Sized Blimp. No offense, Honey, but I couldn't help noticing. It's not healthy. It's no good for you, no kind of way. Don't you have any family or someone in this town to help you out, kid? Someone to help you pull yourself together? Family, like, that's what you need, kid."

"I'm an orphan." That is what I say, and I smile.

She pretends not to hear any of it. She does not seem to see. Instead she mutters when the man goes, tugs at my sleeves. "Listen," she says, "you just have no idea how cruel . . ."

I am about to say "I'm sorry." Again. "Sorry, sorry, sorry." But my breathing is becoming shorter and shorter. I am gasping for air. I feel my face getting blue with the effort, and then I scream it out. I blow the words out.

"What do you want?" I shriek. "What?"

People stop to look. "I must tell you," she says. "You must hear about the very last night before he left. You will not believe this."

"Look," I pant, "I want you to stop following me. I cannot breathe."

"But you are my own child," she says. You, of all people must understand."

"I want you to let go of me," I hiss. "Let go!"

"You are mean," she says. "Oh, yes, mean. Mean like him."

"No," I say. "You are the one who is mean. You hold on, and make me hate you."

"Pity on us," she begins.

"No." I scream. "I need no pity. Let go of me. I am bloated with your sadness. Don't you see? I am too bloated to move comfortably."

"You eat too much," she says without interest. "Look at me. I watch everything I put into my mouth."

"I want to fly." I say it flatly, without enthusiasm.

"Ah," she says smugly, "but you are too fat to fly. You have gotten too fat."

"Not for long," I begin.

"When you were little," she says, "when you were just a little girl, you were my life, do you know that? My whole life. You . . ."

"I am grown up. I want to go away from you."

"A favour," she says. "Could you just . . ." Her face is a child's face now, vulnerable, almost sweet.

"No," I say. "I'm sorry. You will have to find your own way. I cannot help you anymore. It is time for me now. Do you understand?"

"Go then," she says. "They grow up and leave you," she hisses.

"You will be fine," I say to her. "You will be better without me."

"Oh, but . . ." she begins.

"You will be fine," I repeat. "If you try, you will be fine."

Before she can answer, I start running. I run to the end of the tunnel, and then, as the light floods my eyes, almost blinding me, I open my eyes wide, and feel myself rise in the air.

ACKNOWLEDGEMENTS

"Pacing" appeared in *Fiddlehead*. "Woman-Eyes" and "Sugar" appeared in *Event*. "The Helper" appeared in the anthology *Matinees Daily*, edited by Terence Byrnes. "Rice Castle" appeared in *Zymergy*. "Song for a Deaf Man and His Mute Daughter" appeared in *Grain*.